"Did you know your bra is transparent when it's wet?"

Granger McMasters stood beside the pool, regarding her with interest. Melissa ducked under the water. "What are *you* doing here?" she gasped.

"I live here. How about you? Do you just . . . float around, so to speak?"

His appraising look made her furious. She wanted to splash water on his perfectly tailored slacks, his creamy silk shirt and the thin gold watch that alone would have solved all her money problems. She gritted her teeth. "Will you please turn around so I can get out?"

"I rather like the view."

She had a choice: stay in the pool and shrivel up, or get out in her revealing underwear. Not that it was a big deal to *him*. He'd seen countless women in a lot less.

He reached down to pull her out, his masculine hands strong on her bare flesh. . . .

D1013988

Dear Reader,

Welcome to Silhouette **Special Edition** . . . welcome to romance. Each month, Silhouette **Special Edition** publishes six novels with you in mind—stories of love and life, tales that you can identify with—romance with that little "something special" added in.

June has some wonderful stories in bloom for you. Don't miss *Silent Sam's Salvation*—the continuation of Myrna Temte's exciting *Cowboy Country* series. Sam Dawson might not possess the gift of gab, but Dani Smith quickly discovers that still waters run deep—and that she wants to dive right in! Don't miss this tender tale.

Rounding out this month are more stories by some of your favorite authors: Tracy Sinclair, Christine Flynn, Trisha Alexander (with her second book for Silhouette **Special Edition**—remember *Cinderella Girl,* SE #640?), Lucy Gordon and Emilie Richards.

In each Silhouette **Special Edition** novel, we're dedicated to bringing you the romances that you dream about—stories that will delight as well as bring a tear to the eye. And that's what Silhouette **Special Edition** is all about—special books by special authors for special readers!

I hope you enjoy this book and all of the stories to come!

Sincerely,

Tara Gavin
Senior Editor
Silhouette Books

TRACY SINCLAIR
Dreamboat of the Western World

Silhouette Special Edition

Published by Silhouette Books New York

America's Publisher of Contemporary Romance

SILHOUETTE BOOKS
300 East 42nd St., New York, N.Y. 10017

DREAMBOAT OF THE WESTERN WORLD

Copyright © 1992 by Tracy Sinclair

ISBN: 0-373-09746-8

First Silhouette Books printing June 1992

All the characters in this book have no existence outside the imagination of the author and have no relation whatsoever to anyone bearing the same name or names. They are not even distantly inspired by any individual known or unknown to the author, and all incidents are pure invention.

®: Trademark used under license and registered in the United States Patent and Trademark Office and in other countries.

Printed in the U.S.A.

Books by Tracy Sinclair

TRACY SINCLAIR,

author of more than thirty Silhouette novels, also contributes to various magazines and newspapers. An extensive traveler and a dedicated volunteer worker, this California resident has accumulated countless fascinating experiences, settings and acquaintances to draw on in plotting her romances.

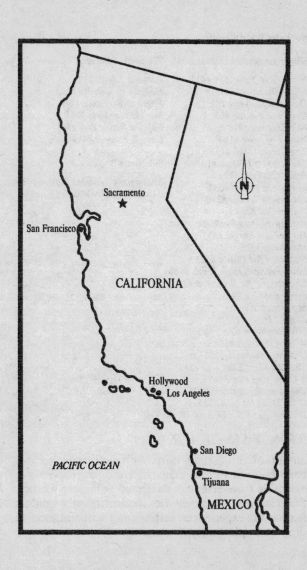

Chapter One

"Where's your sweater?" Melissa Fairfield asked her daughter. "The school bus will be here any minute."

"I'll get it." Betsy Fairfield ran to her room, blond ponytail flying. She called over her shoulder, "You have to sign a slip so I can go with my class to the zoo today."

"Why didn't you tell me last night?"

"I forgot." Betsy reappeared, digging a paper out of her pocket.

Melissa scribbled her name hastily as a horn honked outside. She hugged her daughter's slight body. "There's the bus. Have a good day, honey."

Betsy raced for the door, almost colliding with a woman on the other side. "Sorry, Miss Stoddard. See you later."

Vivian Stoddard laughed as she came in and closed the door. "I was never in that big a hurry to get to school when *I* was seven years old."

"Her class is going to the zoo today," Melissa said. "What's that in your hand?"

Vivian looked ruefully at the small, droopy plant she was carrying. "It started life as an African violet."

"I'm afraid it's ready for the last rites."

"I thought you could give it first aid. You're a professional gardener."

"I don't do house plants."

"I'm sorry I don't have extensive grounds like you're used to," Vivian said dryly.

"It would cost you." Melissa smiled. "I don't work cheap."

"It's hard to believe that you do manual labor for a living."

Vivian's incredulity was valid. Melissa had the face of a Botticelli angel, deep blue eyes, delicate features and framed by long hair the color of honey. Her slender figure was definitely twentieth century, however. Instead of voluptuous curves, she had small, high breasts and a tiny waist.

"I always liked to garden. The difference is that now I get paid for it," Melissa said dismissively. "Do you have time for a cup of coffee?"

"I'd love one. I don't go in until noon today."

"Your hours are almost as flexible as mine," Melissa remarked, leading the way to the kitchen.

"Except that I'm not my own boss like you are." When they were seated at the kitchen table, Vivian asked, "Whose gorgeous estate are you manicuring today?"

"I have a new client—Granger McMasters."

"The movie star?" Vivian's eyes lit up. "How did you get so lucky? He's gorgeous!"

Melissa shrugged. "The only thing about him that interests me is whether he pays his bills on time. You wouldn't believe how long some rich people make you wait for your money."

Vivian brushed that aside. "I know you're down on men in general, but even *you* have to admit that Granger McMasters is a hunk. I always did go for that dark, lean type."

"He keeps in shape by chasing women," Melissa said derisively. "A different one every week."

Vivian sighed ecstatically. "I'd settle for a week with him."

"Forget it. There's something wrong with men who have to keep proving their virility. I know. My ex-husband wrote the book on playing around."

"Just because Stan was a rat doesn't mean all men are. You never give any of them a chance."

"Stan gave me a liberal education," Melissa answered crisply.

"I'm sure it's humiliating to have a man walk out on you," Vivian said tentatively.

"That part was a relief. What I can't forgive is his utter callousness toward his daughter. Stan has never paid one dime of child support." Melissa's eyes sparkled with ongoing resentment. "How did he think I was going to support Betsy?"

"Who needs the jerk? You're doing a great job," Vivian soothed.

"We're only getting by." Melissa propped her head on one hand. "There always seem to be unexpected expenses. I have nightmares wondering what would happen if I couldn't work for some reason. When you're self-employed, you don't have the benefits that come with a regular job."

"Maybe you should consider looking into one."

"How can I and still be here when Betsy comes home from school? If I paid a sitter, I wouldn't wind up with enough to live on."

Vivian considered the insoluble problem. "Well, don't borrow trouble. Nothing's going to happen to you."

"You're right. What am I worried about?" Melissa managed a smile. "This McMasters job is a plum. I'll be going there three times a week."

"What's he like?" Vivian asked eagerly. "Is he as handsome in person?"

"I wouldn't know. I've never met him, and I don't expect to."

"How did you get the job? Didn't he interview you?"

"That's for ordinary people. His business manager handles all the hiring and firing."

"Well, maybe you'll run into Granger accidentally." Vivian gazed critically at Melissa's jeans and T-shirt. "Too bad you can't wear something more glamorous."

"The only thing I'm going to run into are rhododendrons and azalea bushes." Melissa picked up their coffee mugs and carried them to the sink.

"That reminds me. Do you have any suggestions for this?" Vivian held out the African violet.

"I'd give it a decent burial."

The McMasters house occupied almost a full block in the choicest part of Beverly Hills. The beautiful corner mansion faced Sunset Boulevard, but the service entrance was on Terrace Drive. A tall iron fence surrounded the entire property. Melissa stopped her car at the service gate and rang the bell.

After a few moments an intercom that was set into the wall crackled. "Who is it?" a woman's voice asked.

"The gardener," Melissa answered.

"*Who* did you say?"

"I'm the new gardener," Melissa repeated, suppressing a sigh. Where was it written that certain jobs had to be filled by a male?

The electric gate swung open slowly and when Melissa drove her old car up to the back door the woman was waiting for her. After taking a good look at her, the woman's suspicions were confirmed.

"I should have known better than to fall for a trick like that." She was a middle-aged employee wearing a white uniform. "Well, it won't work. You can just turn around and get out of here before I call the police."

"I really am the gardener. William Waxman hired me. You can check with him if you like."

"He didn't say anything to me. I'm Mrs. Flannery, the housekeeper." She looked Melissa up and down. "If you're who you say you are, where's your lawn mower?"

"I have a man who cuts the grass. He'll be here tomorrow. I take care of the plants. Here, I'll give you one of my cards." Melissa reached into her purse.

The woman's belligerence lessened somewhat as she scanned the business card. "Well, I guess you're all right," she said grudgingly. "But I can't be too careful. You have no idea the number of women who try to sneak in here to get a glimpse of Mr. McMasters."

"I suppose it's a problem," Melissa murmured politely.

"That's putting it mildly. They steal everything they can get their hands on for souvenirs. Things you wouldn't believe, like gravel out of the driveway. We finally had to pave it."

"It must be rough to be so popular," Melissa said ironically as she opened the trunk to get out her equipment.

"Mr. McMasters's last picture was the top money-maker for five weeks," Mrs. Flannery informed her proudly.

"That's nice." Melissa slung a large spray tank over her shoulder and walked away.

"How long will you be here?" the housekeeper called.

"All day, but I won't be in your way."

"I'm leaving here soon, so you'll have to let yourself out. Be sure the gate is closed good and tight." Mrs. Flannery obviously still had reservations because she added, "Don't try and get into the house. I turn on the alarm system when I leave, and it's wired right to the police station."

"Mr. McMasters's silver is safe with me," Melissa assured her. "And so are his other jewels."

"I wasn't suggesting you'd steal anything." The woman had the grace to be embarrassed. "I just thought I ought to warn you in case you tried to go inside for a drink of water or something."

"I always carry a thermos."

After she got rid of the housekeeper, Melissa made a tour of the yard. In the center was the requisite Holly-wood swimming pool, complete with a cabana for changing and lounging in the shade. Beyond the flag-stone surrounding the pool area, lush green lawns resembled emerald carpeting. Tall trees provided privacy all along the fence line, and in front of them were flowering bushes and bedding plants.

The previous gardener had done a sloppy job. Many of the bushes needed pruning or thinning out, and Melissa noticed aphids on the primroses.

"I'm going to earn every nickle I charge for this place," she said to herself as she started to pinch off faded camellia blooms.

Melissa was too busy to notice the heat at first, but after several hours of getting up and down off her knees and toting around the heavy spray tank, she felt hot and sticky. The swimming pool beckoned like a shimmering siren.

After trying unsuccessfully to ignore it, she thought, well, why not? It wasn't as though she'd be ripping off her employer. This was a contract job. She was hired to put the grounds into shape and keep them that way. She didn't work by the hour. The housekeeper was gone for the day, and no one could see into the property. After failing to find any reason why she shouldn't, Melissa stripped off her T-shirt and jeans by the side of the pool.

The cool water felt heavenly after the initial shock. She swam the length of the pool several times, then floated on her back, gazing up at the cloudless blue sky. A deep male voice dispelled her reverie.

"Did you know your underwear is transparent when it's wet?" Granger McMasters was standing by the side of the pool looking at her with interest.

Melissa gasped and ducked her body under the water hurriedly. "What are *you* doing here?"

"I live here. How about you? Do you have a home, or do you just float around, so to speak."

"Of course I have a home!"

"You'll admit it was a valid question under the circumstances."

"I'm not one of your crazed fans, if that's what's worrying you," she said scornfully.

"I'm sorry to hear that." He folded his arms over his broad chest and gazed down at her. "Didn't you like my last picture? The critics were very generous."

Melissa wanted to splash water on his perfectly tailored, fawn-colored slacks. Granger was a picture of casual chic. His cream-colored silk shirt was open at the neck, and the sleeves were rolled partly up his muscular forearms. An alligator belt cinched his narrow waist, and on his left wrist was a thin gold watch that would have solved all her money problems.

"Perhaps you're not a movie buff," he said in a conversational tone of voice. "Is that it? I realize a lot of people prefer television."

Melissa gritted her teeth as she treaded water. "Will you please turn around so I can get out?"

"I like the view from here." He grinned.

She was faced with a difficult choice, since Granger seemed set for the day. She could stay in the pool and shrivel up like a raisin, or she could face the ignominy of getting out in her revealing underwear. Not that it was a big deal to him. He'd seen women in a lot less. The appraising look on his face made her furious.

When she swam over to the edge, he held out his hand to help her up. She ignored it, then had to suffer the indignity of letting him help her after all. The stairs were on the opposite side of the pool, but her clothes were on this side, and she couldn't haul herself over the edge. She was sprawled half in and half out of the pool in an ungainly position.

Granger reached down and pulled her to her feet with a hand under each arm. By the time she was standing, with her hair streaming water, Melissa was red with embarrassment and annoyance—and something else. His strong hands on her bare skin were definitely masculine, like the scrutiny he was giving her body. She snatched up her clothes to shield herself.

"I hope you won't think I'm being nosy, but would you mind telling me what you were doing in my pool?" he asked.

"I got warm," she muttered.

"I knew there had to be a logical explanation," he said ironically. "Who are you?"

"I'm the gardener."

His eyes traveled over what he could see of her delicately boned body. "And I'm a plumber."

"It's always good to have a trade to fall back on," she remarked tartly.

"Meaning I'm going to need one?" White teeth gleamed in his deep tan as he laughed.

"You said it, I didn't." Melissa backed away. "I'm going to get dressed."

"You can't put your clothes on over wet underthings. Why don't you dry off first?"

"You must be kidding!" She could have told him the heat from her body was drying her underwear rapidly.

"At least let me give you a towel."

She followed reluctantly as he led her to a dressing room at the side of the cabana, then came inside and handed her a towel. She could have gotten one for herself. They were stacked on a shelf in plain view.

"It might be a good idea if you took off your panties and bra and hung them over a chaise to dry," he remarked.

"That won't be necessary," she said, backing away.

"Are you always this modest?"

"That must be a novelty to you," she answered witheringly.

"It's a virtue that's in rather short supply in this town," he admitted.

"Only among the women *you* know."

He leaned against the wall, regarding her speculatively. "Are you acquainted with them? You still haven't told me your name."

Melissa clutched her clothes more tightly. She had never felt so vulnerable in her life, although Granger was no threat—except to her peace of mind.

"If you'll just go away and let me get dressed, I'll answer all your questions," she said plaintively.

He looked amused at her discomfort. "Okay, I'll make us a drink, and then you can bare your soul—if nothing else."

"I don't want a drink."

"A teetotaler, too. What other virtues do you possess?" he asked mockingly.

"One thing I *don't* have is unlimited patience," she snapped.

"I'm glad to hear you're not perfect." He chuckled. "Although, from what I've seen, you're uncommonly blessed." Before she could erupt he asked, "How about a glass of lemonade?"

"That would be fine." She was forced to accept, otherwise he would never leave.

After Granger had mercifully departed, Melissa scrambled into her clothes. At least she was finally decent, if not very presentable. She combed her fingers through her long hair, but it didn't help much. She still looked disheveled, especially in contrast to Granger's sartorial splendor. His clothes were elegant, his haircut was perfect—the man was unreal! She ignored the memory of his strong hands on her arms, telling her he was *very* real.

Granger was sitting in a wrought-iron chair by an umbrella table when she emerged. He glanced over with a smile. "Do you feel better now?"

"Much better."

"Good." He poured lemonade into a tall glass and handed it to her. "Sit down and let's talk."

Melissa wanted to beg off, but she had to convince him that she was a responsible person. The impromptu dip in his pool hadn't done much for her image.

"Suppose you start with your name," he prompted. "Then we'll get to the part about what you're doing here."

After supplying her name, she said, "I really am your gardener. Mr. Waxman hired me. I'm a very good worker, and I don't usually do impulsive things like I did today. But I wasn't ripping you off," she said earnestly. "I get a flat fee. I don't charge by the hour."

He was looking at her incredulously. "You could scarcely be making this up, but why would you choose to do this kind of work?"

"It pays well." She smiled impishly. "Wait till you get your bill."

"I'm sure you could make more in some other field. Especially with that face and figure."

Her smile died. "I'm not interested in selling either one."

"You know that's not what I meant," he said impatiently. "Why would you choose to do physical labor?"

"I've always liked to garden. It's nice to work outdoors."

"All alone?"

"I don't mind. I usually bring a small radio with me. You'd be surprised at how fast the time passes. I really enjoy working on beautiful grounds like yours."

He was trying to understand. "So this is sort of a hobby?"

"Not unless you also consider eating a hobby," she answered dryly.

"Without seeing my bill, I'll still bet you could make more money at a regular job."

"This is the only thing I'm good at."

"I doubt that." Granger's scrutiny turned frankly male as he gazed at her. The sun was drying her hair to a spun gold nimbus around her delicate face, accentuating blue eyes fringed with darker gold lashes.

"Believe it." She ignored his deepened tone. "I don't type, computers are a mystery to me, and I couldn't sell ten-dollar bills at half off."

"You were never interested in a career?"

She'd never had a chance to prepare for one. Betsy had been conceived a month after she and Stan were married, and he expected her to stay home and take care of the baby. She had no option, since money was scarce and Stan was no help. Melissa wasn't about to tell Granger the story of her life, however.

"Call me a late bloomer," she answered tersely, pushing her chair back. "Thanks for the lemonade. I'll get back to work now."

"What's the rush? You said you don't work by the hour."

"I leave at three."

Granger consulted his handsome watch. "It's only a little after two."

"I have to finish thinning out the camellia bushes."

"They can wait till next time. Do you come every week?"

"I'll be here three times a week. That really isn't too often," she said defensively. "It takes that much time just to maintain a place this size."

"I wasn't complaining," he answered mildly.

Perhaps not now, but she wanted to be sure he understood why the grounds wouldn't reflect her efforts for a while. "Your last gardener did a slipshod job. I'll have to spend weeks catching up on work he neglected to do."

"Then there's no hurry. Why don't you knock off for the day? Stay here and keep me company."

"I'm sure you don't have any trouble finding companionship," she replied evenly. Without waiting for an answer, she started toward the garden.

Granger didn't dispute the charge, but he fell into step beside her. "Do you start early in the morning?"

"I'd like to, but people don't want me to come before nine-thirty or ten."

"So you work from roughly ten until three," he mused. "Those are banker's hours."

"I work straight through with only about ten minutes for lunch and no coffee breaks." She managed a slight laugh. "Today was unusual, but normally I put in almost an average day."

"Where do you go at three? To another job?"

"No, I go home."

"What happens after three o'clock?" he asked. "I've heard of soap opera addicts. You don't want to miss your favorite soap?"

"You couldn't possibly be interested in what I do on my own time."

"You're wrong. It stems from being an actor. I like to know what makes people tick, to get inside their heads, so to speak. That way I can give an accurate portrayal."

"You'd scarcely be called upon to portray someone like me." They'd reached the spot where Melissa had stopped working. She picked up a pair of long pruning shears and began to clip a bush.

"Then perhaps I simply want to know more about you," he said.

"Mr. Waxman can tell you anything you want to know. He interviewed me."

"Bill is very susceptible to beautiful women," Granger said. "I imagine you had the job as soon as you walked in the door."

"It's lucky I didn't have to get *your* approval," Melissa muttered.

"I don't claim to be immune—merely more cautious. You're rather evasive about a number of things."

She looked at him in exasperation. "What is it you suspect me of, Mr. McMasters? I assured your housekeeper that I wasn't here to steal the silver."

"I don't think you're a thief," he answered calmly.

"Then what's bothering you?"

"I'm wondering if you could be a writer for one of the tabloids. They'll do anything to get a story on me. I don't know why." His firm mouth curved contemptuously. "They simply make up stories when they can't get anything juicy enough."

"Are you saying the things they write about you aren't true?"

"I wouldn't ever get a picture made if I spent as much time in bed as they claim."

Melissa was skeptical. "You'd have grounds for a lawsuit if they printed out-and-out falsehoods."

"That would only give the lie wider exposure. The best thing to do is ignore it."

"Doesn't it bother you that you come out looking like a womanizer?"

He smiled thinly. "That's considered macho in our society."

"Tell me!" Melissa's soft mouth set grimly as she raised the shears and began clipping viciously. "I've always wondered what was so great about a man who had to prove his virility by being promiscuous."

"You sound as if you're speaking from experience," Granger remarked casually.

She regretted her moment of self-indulgence. "Everyone knows at least one Don Juan type," she replied carelessly.

"I suppose so." He wasn't convinced, but he didn't pursue the matter.

"Anyway, you have nothing to worry about. I'm neither a writer nor a paid informer. I wish I *were* a writer. I hear studios pay big money for movie scripts."

"You don't happen to have a manuscript that you'd like me to read?" he asked warily.

"No, of course not. Did anyone ever tell you that you have a very suspicious nature?"

"It comes with the territory." He sighed. "You'd be astonished at the number of people who think I can use my influence for them."

"I wouldn't be at all surprised. A lot of people move to Los Angeles hoping to get into show business."

"But not you?"

Melissa shook her head. "My ambition doesn't involve glamour. At least not the kind we're talking about."

"What's your ambition?"

"I'd like to be a landscape architect."

"How is that different from your present occupation?" he asked.

"What I do doesn't require the same training. Architects draw up plans for the landscaping in parks and around public and private buildings. Your grounds were laid out by a specialist. It's a real profession."

"Why don't you get into it?"

"You need a degree, plus graduate study. I didn't finish college."

Actually she'd never even started, but Melissa was reluctant to mention the fact. She couldn't really regret missing out on the opportunity, since Betsy was the consolation prize. She was worth any sacrifice. At the time Melissa had only expected to postpone her education, but Stan hadn't been supportive. And when he walked out, the dream had to be put on hold indefinitely.

"You can go back to school and get your degree," Granger said. "They have night courses."

"Maybe I will someday," she said vaguely.

"Life is too short to put anything off. Why don't you phone this afternoon and sign up for classes?"

"It, uh, isn't convenient right now."

"I suppose you *would* have to give up some of your social life."

She was stung by his openly mocking tone. "My social life has nothing to do with it! As a matter of fact, I don't have any."

"That's hard to believe." His eyes traveled over the upward tilt of her firm breasts. They strained provocatively against her T-shirt as she reached over her head to clip a wayward branch. "A beautiful woman like you must have to fight men off with a stick."

"That would be my preferred method," she muttered under her breath.

Granger heard the comment. "You don't like men?"

"I haven't known very many," she answered evasively. "My experience with the opposite sex isn't as wide as yours."

"I'm older than you." He smiled.

"I don't think I could ever catch up," she remarked dryly. Then, to keep him talking about himself so he'd stop questioning *her,* she asked, "Are you and Felicia

Grant still a happy couple?'' She was the current female superstar.

"You've been reading the tabloids at the market checkout counters," he answered mockingly.

"It's escapism. We all like to live vicariously with the rich and famous."

"Do you know what I plan to do tonight?" Without giving her a chance to reply, he continued. "I'm going to heat up whatever Mrs. Flannery left for me in the refrigerator, and then I'll read scripts the rest of the evening. Doesn't that sound glamorous?"

"I suppose even celebrities get tired of running around every night."

"I spend more nights like this than you'd imagine."

"Only by choice. Don't expect me to believe you couldn't get a date if you wanted one."

"You're right. But I don't want to go to fancy restaurants and nightclubs every night." He jammed his hands into his pockets and frowned. "Normal people stay home and play bridge with their friends, or just sit and have a conversation."

Melissa smiled. "You've evidently never heard of the boob tube. That's where ordinary people spend most of their time, parked in front of the television set."

"Some, but not all. Before I got to be a so-called star, I took a date to the movies, or we cooked dinner together at home and talked for hours."

"You could still do that."

"Hardly. The women I know want to be seen at all the best places. They'd be a trifle conspicuous at the movies in a Mackie gown cut to the navel."

"The answer is simple," Melissa said crisply. "Get some new girlfriends."

"Where do I find them? I can't walk up to a stranger and ask, 'Would you like to have a pizza and go for a walk along the beach?'"

"I'll bet you wouldn't get turned down." She grinned.

"You know what I'm saying."

Melissa tossed her shears on the ground and brushed the hair off her forehead with one forearm. Glancing around at the elegant house and spacious grounds, she raised an eyebrow. "Are you asking me to feel sorry for you?"

"No, of course not. I'm very lucky, and I know it. I'm only telling you that it's possible to be rich and lonely at the same time."

The appealing, little-boy expression on his face was incongruous, considering his powerful frame and handsome, rugged features. Still, Melissa couldn't help softening toward him. She knew what it was like to be lonely.

"You don't have to approach strangers," she said more gently. "I'm sure you come in contact with a lot of nice, normal women who would be thrilled to go to the movies with you and share a pizza."

"How about you? Will you have dinner with me tonight?"

Her sympathy shriveled and died. "That's about the most devious come-on I've ever been subjected to."

"Why would you think such a thing?"

"It's perfectly obvious." Her blue eyes were stormy. "You happen to find yourself at loose ends one night, so you decide to amuse yourself with the hired help."

"Now who has the suspicious nature?" he asked quietly.

"I have every right to be suspicious. Why would you ask *me* out?"

"Because you're quite lovely, and you treat me like a person. Not one you like very much, but we can work on that," he said calmly.

"I hate to puncture your confidence, but I'm not going out with you—ever."

"Why?"

"Because we have absolutely nothing in common, for starters."

"How do you know that? We've spent less than an hour together. Maybe we have a great deal in common. How do you feel about lima beans?"

"I love them."

"So do I. See, that's a beginning."

"Most people hate lima beans," she said skeptically. "You would have agreed with me no matter what I said."

"I'll prove you're wrong. Ask me the same kind of question."

She thought for a minute. "How do you feel about dogs?"

"I love them," he answered promptly. "If you say you hate them, I'm going to start having serious doubts about us."

"No, I love them," she admitted.

"What's your favorite breed?" he asked.

"There aren't any dogs I don't like, but I'm partial to black standard poodles."

"They're awesomely intelligent," he agreed.

"You have all of this space. Why don't you have a dog? I'd have several if I lived here."

"I considered it, but I'm gone so much of the time. It doesn't seem fair to an animal. You owe a living creature love and companionship, not just food and shelter."

Melissa wouldn't have expected such sensitivity from a man whose life seemed totally hedonistic. Was she wrong about him? Maybe she *had* been unfair.

"Won't you reconsider and have dinner with me?" he urged. "I'll take you anywhere you want to go, or if you'd rather stay here, I have some outtakes from movies that are very funny. I promise you won't be bored."

"I'm on to you." She smiled. "You just want someone to cook your dinner."

"You won't have to lift a finger," he promised. "Mrs. Flannery isn't the warmest person around, but she's a great cook. I'll serve and clean up afterward."

"Are you trying to tell me that Granger McMasters, star of stage, screen and television knows how to wash dishes?" she teased.

"There's a great new invention called a dishwasher. Even your average bit player can operate one."

"I'll bet you just pile the dishes in the sink and leave them," she said.

"Did the *National Observer* print that, too?"

Melissa hadn't felt this lighthearted in years—or this desirable. She knew better than to believe Granger was interested in her in more than a passing way. Surrounded as he was by the world's most gorgeous women, how could he be? But even a knee-jerk reaction from a man like him was flattering.

Not because he was a big star. Granger could make a woman feel special without needing outside help. His combination of virility and an underlying hint of gentleness carried a powerful wallop. Melissa found herself wondering what it would be like to feel that taut body covering hers, his face poised over her in the darkness.

She dispelled the erotic fantasy by laughing breathlessly. "You see why people read the tabloids? Where else could I find out such personal things about you?"

He smiled meltingly. "Have dinner with me, and I'll tell you anything you want to know."

As she stared up at him, noticing how thick his eyelashes were, a group of people came around a corner of the house.

"Doesn't Flannery answer the doorbell anymore?" a man called. "Your car is in the driveway, so we knew you were home."

Granger suppressed a flash of annoyance as he turned to the newcomers. "Hi, Sid. What brings you here in the middle of the afternoon?"

Felicia Grant walked toward him, as stunningly beautiful as she was on the screen. "We just finished lunch at the Polo Lounge, and we're looking for some excitement." She reached Granger and lifted her face expectantly to his.

He pecked her on the cheek. "You've come to the wrong place. I plan to take a swim and then wade through a stack of scripts."

She wrinkled her perfectly shaped nose. "If they're anything like the ones the studio sent *me,* you're wasting your time."

"I'm not so sure. One of them looks promising."

"Hey, Granger, what do you have to do to get a drink around here?" another of the men called.

"You know where the bar is." Granger's voice held an ironic undertone.

Sid joined him and Felicia, glancing at Melissa approvingly. "Not bad. If I could get help like that, I'd trade my condo for a house."

Granger's expression was austere. "Melissa, I'd like you to meet Felicia Grant and Sid Blackman."

Melissa was stuffing clippings into a large plastic bag. She looked up briefly and nodded, too angry to speak. The man, Sid, was not only treating her like a sex object, but a deaf and dumb one as well!

After an equally brief nod, Felicia said to Granger, "Let's drive down to Malibu and drop in on Solly. He always has a fun group around."

Melissa closed the plastic bag with a final, vicious twist. Hoisting it into her arms, she walked away with a straight back.

Granger followed her. "Let me carry that for you."

"I can do it," she answered curtly. "This is what I get paid for."

After a look at her stony face he didn't insist, but he continued to walk alongside her. "I must apologize for Sid. His manners leave a lot to be desired."

"It isn't important."

"Not when you consider the source." He paused, slanting a glance at her. "Do we have a date tonight?"

"Don't worry, I had no intention of accepting." They had reached Melissa's car. She dumped the bag in the trunk and banged it shut with unnecessary force. "You can go to Malibu with a clear conscience."

"I don't want to go to Malibu. I want to have dinner with you."

"That's as truthful as your story about being lonely." She climbed into her car and started the motor. "You're a really great actor, Mr. McMasters. I almost believed you."

Melissa was furious with herself as she drove away. How could she have let her guard down like that? All it took was a little sweet talk, and she was as gullible as a teenager. Granger had merely been practicing his seductive technique. Her first evaluation of him was correct. He was no more trustworthy than any other man.

Chapter Two

Melissa put all thoughts of Granger out of her mind when Betsy got home. Her daughter made that easy. She was always bubbling over with the day's events.

Melissa gazed fondly at the small girl's animated face. Everyone said they looked alike, but people often said that about mothers and daughters. Betsy's hair was a pale blond, as opposed to Melissa's deeper honey color, and her eyes were a velvety brown, rather than blue. Luckily that was her only legacy from Stan. Besides being beautiful, she was a delightful child. Complete strangers had made a fuss over her since she was a baby.

Betsy finished recounting her day at the zoo. "I wish we could have a tiger cub. They're so cute."

"Unfortunately they don't stay little and cuddly." Melissa smiled.

"Well then, can we have a dog?"

"We discussed that, honey. You know the landlord doesn't allow pets."

"Even a little teeny puppy?"

"I'm afraid not. Did you have lunch at the zoo?" Melissa asked to distract her.

"Uh-huh. I traded my apple to Cathy for her orange." Betsy took a gulp of milk before going off on a tangent. "Can we go to Hawaii this summer? Cathy's parents are taking her. They'll be gone for a whole month."

"I wish we could, but we can't afford it." Melissa had always been honest with her about their finances, and Betsy had accepted the situation with a maturity beyond her years.

"I told her I didn't think we could go," Betsy remarked matter-of-factly. "She said we could if you married a rich man. Then we could do all kinds of things."

"Did Cathy think of that solution by herself?" Melissa asked dryly.

"No, her mother told her."

"I thought so."

Betsy looked at her curiously. "If you married a rich man, would he be my daddy?"

"Technically he'd be your stepfather."

"Is that like the wicked stepmother in Cinderella?" The little girl looked apprehensive. "I wouldn't like that."

"You have nothing to worry about." Melissa hugged her close. "I'm not going to marry anybody."

After they'd had dinner and Betsy was in bed, Melissa turned on the television set. She switched channels several times, but nothing held her interest. For some reason she felt unusually restless. It was a relief when Vivian stopped by, still in her nurse's uniform.

"I couldn't wait to find out about Granger Mc-Masters," she said. "How was your first day on the job?"

Melissa shrugged. "Like any other day."

"How can you be so blasé? Did you get inside the house? Does he have a million servants?"

"As far as I know he roughs it with only a house-keeper, who doubles as a guard dog. She thinks he's the greatest thing since the invention of tax shelters."

"She's right. Imagine working for Granger Mc-Masters and getting to see him every day. If he ever needs a nurse, be sure and recommend me. I wouldn't mind giving him a sponge bath." Vivian grinned.

"Forget it. He's the healthiest looking man I've ever seen—all muscle, including the one between his ears."

"You got to *see* him?" Vivian breathed.

Actually, he'd gotten to see more of *her,* Melissa thought ruefully, remembering the embarrassing incident in the pool. She had no intention of telling Vivian about that.

"He happened to come home while I was working," she answered dismissively.

"And? Don't keep me in suspense. Is he as gorgeous in person?"

"If you like the type. He looks the same as he does in the movies."

"No elevator shoes or a hairpiece?"

"I wouldn't know about the hairpiece, but he's as tall as he looks on the screen."

"Did he talk to you? Tell me every word he said!"

"You're being ridiculous, Vivian," Melissa said impatiently. "He's just a man like any other."

"You've got to be kidding! The guy who fixes your washing machine is just a man. Granger is the stuff dreams are made of."

"And just about as substantial."

"Is this your normal male-bashing talking, or did he do something to put you off?"

"I don't appreciate being used to bolster someone's self-confidence," Melissa replied distantly. "Especially since he already has an ego bigger than Cleveland."

"What does that mean?"

"Nothing. Just forget it."

"Why don't you tell me what happened? You know I'm going to get it out of you."

"Nothing happened," Melissa insisted. "He asked me to have dinner with him, and then Felicia Grant and a bunch of his friends showed up, and that was that."

Vivian couldn't decide which exciting event to ask about first. She settled on the most astounding. "Granger McMasters asked you for a date? That's fantastic! You accepted, of course."

"Do you see him around anywhere?"

"You mean, he wanted to take you out tonight? How could you turn him down?" Vivian groaned.

"I didn't get a chance to. His girlfriend made him a better offer."

"That rat! Of course you *were* up against heavy competition. Felicia Grant is something special. Not that I'm excusing him," Vivian added hurriedly.

"I couldn't care less," Melissa said loftily. "I had no intention of going out with him—tonight or ever."

"Don't be too hasty. Maybe he couldn't get out of dumping you for Felicia."

"Thanks. That makes me feel a lot better."

"Well, you have to be realistic. I hear she's a tough cookie. What Felicia wants, Felicia gets."

"She can have him!"

"Be smart for once. Your life wouldn't exactly make a bestseller. Granger can take you to all the places we only read about. You don't have to fall in love with the guy. In fact, I'd definitely advise against it."

"At least we agree on one thing," Melissa remarked.

"All I'm saying is, take him up on it if he asks you a second time. Do you know what most women would do to be in your shoes?"

"This whole conversation is silly. Granger just happened to come home today, but I'm sure it was an isolated occurrence. I don't expect to see him again."

"I'll bet you will."

Vivian's hunch was correct. When Melissa arrived at the McMaster house on Wednesday, Granger was lying on a chaise by the pool, reading. She paused, staring at him through a gap in the tall hedge screening off the pool area.

Even Melissa had to admit his physique was outstanding. Granger wore only a pair of brief white bathing trunks, which emphasized his deep tan. She wondered if there was a strip of white skin under his trunks, or if he sunbathed in the nude to get his body the same color all over. The fleeting thought annoyed her, along with her behavior. She was acting like a giddy teenager, peeking through the bushes this way.

Melissa would have avoided him, but the only way to the yard was past the pool area. She nodded to him as she crossed the flagstone, hoping he'd give her the same silent treatment. He didn't.

Granger glanced up and smiled. "Good morning. Beautiful day, isn't it?"

"Very nice," she answered, briefly but politely.

"We're lucky. It's always beautiful in Los Angeles."

"I suppose that's why so many people move here," she remarked.

"Is that what brought *you?*"

"No, I was born here."

Melissa felt that she'd fulfilled her conversational obligation. She continued on toward the garden, but she watched him out of the corner of her eye, fascinated in spite of herself. Granger swung his legs to the cement and stood up in one fluid movement, like a giant cat flexing supple muscles.

He came over to walk beside her. "What's your project for today?"

She knew he couldn't care less, but he had a right to ask. "I'm going to pull out the primroses and plant impatiens."

"Are primroses the ones with the pretty flowers?"

"Yes."

"They look nice," he said tentatively.

"The season is almost over. In a couple of weeks they'd get straggly. I rotate the plants before that happens."

"Oh." He was silent for a moment as she knelt down and began uprooting the bedding plants. "Do you mind if I watch?"

"That's your privilege, but you'll find it about as stimulating as watching paint dry," she warned.

"It's better than reading through a stack of terrible scripts," he said ruefully.

"That sounds like fun to me. I love to read."

"So do I, but you can't imagine the garbage they send me. And this is stuff that got past the first reader."

"What's a first reader?"

"Someone who reads submissions and supposedly separates the junk from the jewels."

Melissa sat back on her heels and looked up at him. "There are people who get paid just to read?"

"Not much, but yes, they're paid. Often they're free-lancers who do it in their spare time."

"Could I get a job doing that?" she asked.

He raised an eyebrow. "Are you giving up on me so soon?"

"Not at all. That's something I could do at night."

"Surely you have better things to do with your time."

"I can't think of anything I'd enjoy more, and I'd be making money, too." The extra income would be a god-send.

"Your values are seriously skewed," Granger remarked dryly.

She didn't bother to argue the point. "Would you put in a good word for me at the script department, or wherever?" When he stared at her with a slight frown, not answering immediately, Melissa realized her mistake. "I'm sorry. I shouldn't have asked. You told me how people are always plaguing you for favors, and here I am doing the same thing."

"I don't mind in the least. I'd be happy to recommend you. I was merely wondering why you want to work night and day."

She smiled wryly. "Little luxuries like food cost a fortune nowadays."

"You don't look as if you eat very much." He glanced at her slim waist and rounded bottom.

"I work it off." Melissa went back to uprooting prim-roses.

Granger squatted down beside her. "Do you have an extra trowel? I'll help you. I need to keep in trim, too."

"You're in great shape already," she said frankly, gazing at his broad shoulders and corded leg muscles.

He chuckled. "That's the first nice thing you've ever said to me."

"I've been polite," she protested, hoping he wouldn't remember her occasional lapses.

"That's not the same as being nice."

"I don't imagine you're subjected to much criticism," she answered ironically.

"That doesn't mean I don't enjoy compliments. When they're sincere."

"How do you know I wasn't just buttering you up to get the reading job?"

He turned his head to look at her. "I don't think you have a devious thought in your head."

"That's the first sincere thing *you've* said to *me*." She was incredibly pleased.

"You don't think I meant it when I told you that you're beautiful?"

Melissa's glow faded. "Not compared to Felicia Grant, obviously. Did you have a good time in Malibu?"

"I wouldn't have gone if you'd agreed to have dinner with me."

"You expect me to believe that?" She jabbed the trowel into the ground with unnecessary force.

"How can a woman like you have such low self-esteem?" he asked wonderingly.

"That's not true! I feel great about myself," she flared. "I stand on my own two feet, and I take care of my responsibilities. Not all women need a man to feel secure. I'm happy just the way I am."

Granger regarded her enigmatically. "You don't have to *need* men to go out with them. Whey don't you date?"

Melissa realized she'd revealed too much. She dipped her head so a curtain of hair shielded her from his searching eyes. "I didn't mean to give the impression that I stay home alone every night. Nothing could be farther from the truth."

He reached out and tucked her hair behind her ear. It was an innocent gesture, a simple attempt to see her face while they talked. But the intimate feeling of his long fingers on her skin sent a shiver down Melissa's spine. She had to force herself not to react visibly.

Mercifully, he removed his hand. "Then I have to take your rejection personally. What don't you like about me?"

"It isn't personal at all. I simply make it a rule never to date my employers."

"Why? We don't work in an office. No one's going to accuse you of getting preferential treatment because of it."

"That's not the only danger. Suppose we didn't hit it off? We don't exactly agree on everything. I'm not willing to jeopardize my livelihood for the sake of one dinner."

"In other words, you're afraid I'd fire you if you didn't come across."

Melissa's cheeks turned pink. "That isn't what I said at all."

"It's what you meant. That explains why you tense up whenever I touch you." He stared at her curiously. "Do you honestly think I'd fire you because you refused to go to bed with me?"

"You're the one who brought it up. I never even thought about you that way," she declared.

"I'm crushed." He grinned. "If I said the same about you, I'd be lying."

"That's a good reason for keeping our relationship strictly business," she answered primly.

"I don't see why. What's wrong with combining business and pleasure?"

Melissa knew he was only baiting her, which made her even angrier. "*Your* pleasure or mine?" she snapped.

"I'd try very hard to see that you enjoyed the experience."

His deep velvet voice conjured up visions of arousing kisses and sensuous caresses along the length of her bare body. She knew instinctively that Granger wasn't promising anything he couldn't deliver. It would indeed be a memorable experience.

Taking a deep breath, she asked, "Didn't you say you had work to do?"

"Am I bothering you?" he asked innocently.

"Not in the slightest, but you *are* slowing me down. I have several flats of impatiens to plant today."

"Why didn't you say so?" When he rose to his feet, Melissa breathed a sigh of relief that was short-lived. "Where are they?" he asked. "I'll bring them, and we can get started."

"That's *my* job," she insisted. "You're supposed to be reading scripts."

"I'd rather plant flowers. It's sort of like giving birth to something." He smiled.

"Only a lot easier," she commented dryly.

His interest quickened. "Are you speaking from first-hand experience?"

"The flats are in the back of my car if you really want to help," she answered evasively.

Granger looked at her thoughtfully, but he didn't repeat the question. When he returned with the flats, she didn't give him a chance to resume the subject.

"Make a series of little holes first," she instructed. "Then cut a square around each plant and lift it out with the soil still surrounding the roots."

"They look so puny," he complained.

"All bedding plants start out that way. They'll be lovely in a couple of weeks. Trust me."

"I will if you will," he answered softly.

Without replying, Melissa moved to the farthest end of the flower bed where she uprooted the plants he would replace. She told herself that Granger would tire of the game soon, but he showed no signs of it.

While she worked silently, he kept up a steady flow of conversation—none of it personal, however. He asked her the names of flowers and mentioned a movie he'd made in Hawaii and how lush the foliage had been.

"Have you been there lately?" he asked.

"I've never been to the Islands. My...a friend of mine wanted us to go this summer."

"It can be a trifle humid then. I'd suggest you pick one of the other seasons instead."

"Maybe I will," she said vaguely.

"Let me know when you plan to go. I'll arrange the VIP treatment for you."

"It must be great to be a celebrity," Melissa commented.

"In some respects. It's nice to be met by a limo and not have to hassle your luggage. But celebrity has its downside, too."

"Such as?"

"I can't walk down the street in cutoffs, eating an ice-cream cone. Or have a quiet dinner in a restaurant with friends. Every time I go out it's a media event."

"I guess that *would* be a little annoying."

"Of course there are compensations." He slanted a mischievous glance at her. "The *National Observer* says I get to sleep with any woman I choose. They haven't heard about you."

"Let's keep that our little secret," Melissa said.

"That might be an angle," he mused. "If you don't go out with me, I'll unleash the tabloids on you. I can see the headlines now. 'Shocking reason why Melissa Fairfield spurned Granger McMasters's advances.'"

She laughed. "You wouldn't be that ruthless."

"Don't bet on it. I'll sacrifice anyone to get what I want."

"I don't believe that." Melissa took a short break. Clasping her arms around her raised knees, she gazed at Granger measuringly. "You seem remarkably well adjusted, considering."

"Considering what?"

"That you can have anything you want out of life."

"How about you?"

"I'm good for your character," she answered lightly. "Nobody should have *everything*."

"Now you're changing the rules. You just told me I could."

"It would serve you right if I took you seriously," she warned.

He smiled meltingly. "I keep hoping you will."

"That would take all the fun out of it."

Something flickered in his gray eyes. "On the contrary. The fun would be just beginning," he murmured.

Melissa didn't know if she was angrier at Granger or herself for the surge of excitement he could arouse so effortlessly. "You can get that kind of fun anywhere," she said evenly. "It's more stimulating to take advantage of someone who's defenseless."

His face sobered. "That's a serious accusation. I'll admit to having faults, but I've never taken advantage of a woman in my life."

"What do you call what you're doing to me?" she demanded.

"I didn't realize you were taking this so seriously," he answered slowly.

"You're saying you *don't* want to make love to me?" Instead of relief she felt an illogical twinge of regret.

His smile was back. "I'll say it if it will put your mind at ease, but it wouldn't be true. Of course I want to make love to you. You're a gorgeous woman with a fantastic body."

Melissa had an uncomfortable moment, remembering that he wasn't merely speculating about her body. To make matters worse, he became more explicit.

"I'd like to hold you in my arms and kiss you until you want me as much as I want you. I have a feeling that under all those restraints you put on yourself, you're a very passionate woman."

Had she once been? Certainly Stan had never made her feel like that, except briefly in the beginning. She could imagine all the things Granger was describing. He would make love unselfishly, awakening her almost unbearably with his expertise, then satisfying her completely.

Granger was watching the play of emotions cross her mobile face. He came to stand over her. "What happened, Melissa? Did a man hurt you so badly that you're afraid to trust any of us?"

She scrambled to her feet and busied herself brushing grass off the knees of her jeans. "That's the trouble with the acting profession. You think everybody's life is a motion picture."

He lifted her chin in his hand, forcing her to look at him. "I must have come close if I panicked you like this. Do you want to talk about it?"

"No." Her lowered lashes made shadows on her flushed cheeks.

He smoothed her hair gently. "I'd like to beat the guy to a pulp, whoever he is."

His touch was so gentle. Melissa was almost overcome by the desire to move into Granger's arms and have him hold her close and croon reassuring words in her ear. It had been so long since a man had seemed to care about her as a person.

Luckily the housekeeper appeared on the patio. "Telephone, Mr. McMasters," she called.

By the time Granger returned, Melissa had mastered her momentary weakness. She was prepared to fend off his attempt to tear down her defenses again, but he didn't make any.

"Lunch is almost ready," he remarked casually. "I told Mrs. Flannery we'd eat by the pool."

"Thanks, but I told you, I don't stop for lunch."

"That was before you had an assistant. Even though I was all thumbs, I must have saved you some time."

"You were very helpful," she admitted.

"Then you can take a break for lunch. How about a swim before we eat? Gardening is really sweaty work."

"You go ahead. I'll finish up here," she mumbled.

He looked amused, knowing what was on her mind. "I keep a supply of bathing suits for guests. You'll find them in the dressing room."

Melissa followed instructions, since she was learning that Granger always got his own way. In this case she didn't mind. A swim would feel great.

There was an extensive collection of bathing suits in the cabana, but the only ones in her size were bikinis. The less revealing tank suits were too big. She selected the most demure of the lot, a sky-blue bikini with a ruffle around the top of the bra and another circling the hips.

Granger was already in the pool when Melissa came out. She stood on the edge for a moment, watching in admiration as he sliced through the water with powerful strokes. The same admiration was mirrored in his eyes when he turned his head and saw her.

"That's almost as sexy as your last outfit," he called, swimming over to her.

"Aren't you ever going to forget about that?" she asked plaintively.

"You're asking a lot."

His eyes moved over the gentle curve of her breasts above the brief top, then traveled past her navel to the scrap of blue fabric that hugged her hips. She couldn't take offense because there was no insolence in his gaze, simply open appreciation. It was gratifying and disturbing at the same time. Melissa dived into the pool.

She surfaced beyond Granger and struck out for the deep end. As he swam toward her, she discovered that the bow in the middle of her back had come undone. Her top was attached only by the tie around her neck. It was floating under her chin, leaving her bare breasts exposed.

"Good stroke," Granger called as he swam over to her.

She turned her back to him and struggled to retie her top while treading water.

"What are you doing?" he asked curiously.

"My bra came undone," she gritted.

"Let me help you," he offered.

"No! I can do it." Her words were muffled as the water covered her nose and mouth.

"You're going to drown yourself in the process." His arm curved around her waist, supporting her while she retied the strings.

Melissa breathed a sigh of relief when the job was done. Granger's intentions were no doubt innocent, but she was entirely too conscious of his lithe body cradling hers. There was something sensuous about the water lapping around them, rocking their almost naked bodies against each other.

"Okay, you can let go now," she said.

"Do I have to?" He trailed his lips teasingly across her shoulder. "Who knows when I'll get another opportunity like this?"

"You won't." She pried his arms apart. "I intend to stay out of your pool from now on. Something embarrassing always happens."

"With a figure like yours you have nothing to worry about."

"I'm not as uninhibited as you are."

"We'll definitely have to work on that." Before she could disagree, he said, "Come on, I'll race you to the shallow end."

Melissa struck out with flashing arms and legs, not to try to beat Granger, but as a release from the tension she always felt around him. He kept pace with her, cutting through the water with half her effort.

When they reached the steps, he said, "It's a tie."

"You know better. You could have beaten me easily."

He shrugged. "What would that have proved? I'm bigger and stronger than you."

"Most men like to show off, anyway."

"Another compliment?" He grinned. "Be careful. I might begin to think you care."

"Go ahead. You live in a world of make-believe," she replied lightly.

"Perhaps you should try it. You might get more fun out of life."

"What makes you think my life isn't fun?" This day certainly couldn't be called dull. Melissa rested her head on one of the shallow steps and stretched out her legs, letting the water rock her gently.

Without answering her question, Granger wrapped a strand of her floating hair around his finger. "You look like a mermaid. It's no wonder sailors used to be lured to their destruction when they sighted one."

"Scientists have decided those mythical mermaids were actually manatees. The big, funny-looking mammals we call sea cows."

"Scientists have no romance in their souls. I prefer to think those ancient mariners were seduced by a siren with long golden hair and eyes the color of the sea. Someone who looked like you."

"If she did, sailors in those days must have had poor eyesight. My hair is a mess, and I'm not wearing any makeup."

"You don't need any." He studied her face. "You have exquisite bone structure."

"Next you'll be telling me I belong in pictures," she said derisively.

"Nowadays beauty isn't enough, but if you have acting ability, you might make it big. Maybe you should try it."

"No thanks. I'd rather be a good gardener than a bad actress."

"That makes sense," he admitted. "Ah, here's our lunch."

Mrs. Flannery was wheeling a tea cart onto the terrace. They got out of the pool and dried off with large towels, and Granger pulled on a navy T-shirt.

The housekeeper's disapproval of Melissa as a guest was evident. She ignored her, addressing all her comments to Granger.

"I made your favorite chicken salad, Mr. McMasters. With just a hint of curry the way you like it."

"It looks wonderful." He smiled. "Nobody makes better chicken salad than Mrs. Flannery," he told Melissa.

"I can hardly wait to taste it," she answered demurely. When the woman had gone back into the house, Melissa said, "Mrs. Flannery doesn't think I should be having lunch with you."

"Don't take it personally. She doesn't approve of any of my female friends. If she had her way, I'd live a monkish existence."

"Maybe she's in love with you."

"Good Lord, no! She's more like a mother hen with one chick. She never married, and the only family she has is a brother back East. This job is her whole life. It's rather sad."

"Can you imagine how she'd react if you ever brought home a wife? It's a good thing you don't intend to get married."

"What makes you think I'm a confirmed bachelor?"

"You're giving a good imitation of one. A lot of men in your industry are on their second or third wives by now and still looking."

"I never could understand why they think subsequent marriages will work when the first one failed."

Melissa pushed her chicken salad around the plate. "They say you don't really know someone until you're married to him—or her," she added hurriedly.

"Maybe if you're very young. A mature person knows when it's the real thing."

Her smile was twisted. "You know that for a fact?"

"I suppose I should only speak for myself. When *I* meet the right woman, she'll be my first and only wife."

As Melissa was deciding whether it was worthwhile to challenge Granger's statement, a man came out of the house and started toward them. It was William Waxman, and he looked annoyed.

"I had to drive all the way over here because Flannery refused to call you to the phone," he said irately. "Honestly, Granger, you have to do something about that woman."

"It isn't her fault. I told her to hold my calls," Granger answered.

"It didn't occur to you that something important might come up?"

"We don't always see eye to eye on what's important," Granger replied calmly. "Say hello to Melissa."

The man looked at her for the first time. A slight frown puckered his brow as he tried to place her. "How do you do? I'm Bill Waxman."

"I know." She smiled. "You hired me."

"He doesn't recognize you without your clothes." Granger chuckled. "That proves you got the job on merit alone."

Melissa took pity on the man. "I'm Mr. McMasters's gardener."

His face cleared. "Of course! I remember now. But you did look different in my office."

As his gaze took in her bikini, she felt the need to set the record straight. "It's very unusual for me to take time out for lunch. I don't intend to do it again."

"He doesn't pay your salary, I do." Granger looked at his business manager with more than a hint of irritation. "What's so important that you had to come out here?"

"I was reconciling your bank statement, and there are two checks for very large amounts."

"Am I overdrawn?"

"Certainly not! You have plenty of money to cover them."

"Then what's the problem?" Granger asked.

"You didn't say what they're for."

"What difference does it make? It's my money. I can spend it any way I choose." Granger frowned.

"But I have to know where it went—for income tax purposes," his business manager insisted.

"Charge it to personal expenses."

"Meaning charity." Bill sighed. "You're a pushover for every loser with a sob story."

"People can have a run of bad luck. That doesn't make them losers," Granger said sharply.

"Okay, okay. I stand corrected." Bill held his hands up, palms out. "But you have to admit you've made some . . . um . . . pretty bad investments."

"Big deal. It's only money."

"What am I going to do with this guy?" Bill appealed to Melissa in his frustration. "He can't see that people are taking advantage of him."

"I propose we drop the subject," Granger said curtly. "Do you want lunch?"

"I wouldn't mind."

Granger shoved his chair back and strode toward the kitchen, his straight back registering displeasure.

Bill gazed after him. "You can't win. He hires me to look after his interest, and then gets mad when I try to do my job."

"Granger makes a great deal of money. I think it's admirable that he gives something back," Melissa said.

"I'm not talking about regular charities. I could tell you stories about the people he—" Bill stopped as Granger returned. "I brought another script for you to read," he told him. "Max sent it over. He says this one's a real winner."

"Agents always say that," Granger answered dismissively. "They want their clients to keep working."

"Is that bad?" Bill asked. "How long is this vacation of yours going to last?"

"Until they send me a decent script."

"*Gone with the Wind* has already been done," Bill commented dryly.

"Let's drop it, shall we? I'm sure Melissa finds this boring."

"Not really," she said. "It's interesting to hear how the entertainment industry functions. You get to dictate what you will or won't do?"

"I wouldn't call it dictating," Granger protested.

"But you do have the right to refuse a picture you don't like."

"I'm fortunate in that respect. A studio only has money at stake, but an actor risks his reputation if he does a bad movie," he explained.

Bill chuckled. "Granger can't forget *Spanish Bay,* the flick a producer talked him into against his better judgment."

"They're still airing out the theaters," Granger commented ruefully.

Melissa looked at him curiously. "I can't imagine you ever having a setback."

"You have some strange misconceptions about me. I'm as vulnerable as any other man, I assure you."

She didn't believe that for a minute. Granger was the picture of success: handsome, rich, sought after. He looked invincible, as though nothing or no one could touch him. Certainly not a woman.

"It's time you forgot about that bomb," Bill told Granger. "Just promise you'll read the new script I brought over. I leafed through it, and I think it has possibilities."

"If it involves another crusading attorney or macho cop, forget it."

Melissa was so interested in the inner workings of show business that the time slipped by unnoticed. She was reminded of how long she'd taken off when Bill looked at his watch. It was almost three o'clock!

"This has been charming, but some of us have work to do," he remarked.

"I have to go, too. May I leave the flats in a corner of your garage?" Melissa asked Granger. "I'll finish planting them on Friday."

"Keep an open mind about that script." Bill waved and left them.

Granger followed Melissa into the garden. "Everyone's leaving me," he complained.

"It's a good thing. You've wasted a good part of the day with Bill and me."

"I wouldn't call it wasted. Not with you, anyway."

"You just welcome any opportunity to goof off," she scolded.

He chuckled. "You know what they say about all work and no play."

"There's such a thing as equal time." Melissa glanced at her watch as she bent over to pick up a flat of seedlings.

"I'll put those away," Granger offered.

"No, that's all right. I'll do it."

"I was trying to save you some time. You seem to be in a hurry."

"I really should leave," she said indecisively.

"Then go ahead. Does it take you very long to get home from here?" he asked casually.

"It depends on the traffic. I'll come a little earlier on Friday to make up for the time I took off today. If that's all right with you," she added.

"You don't have to. I might plant a few more of these—what do you call them?"

"Impatiens. But you have your own work to do."

"Are you afraid I'll take over your job?" he teased.

"Not really. Something will come along to distract you. Or some*body*."

Granger walked with her to her car. "You're determined to stereotype me as a Hollywood playboy, aren't you?"

She tossed her tools in the trunk. "You have a right to be anything you like."

"Are you agreeing with me?"

"The customer is always right," she answered lightly. "I'm just trying to be cooperative."

"If that was really your aim, you'd have dinner with me tonight."

She slid behind the wheel. "We had lunch together."

He leaned his crossed arms on the door frame. "You can only take me in small doses?"

Granger's face was just inches from hers. She could see the laughter lines at the corners of his eyes and the tiny white scar on one of his high cheekbones. A makeup man must camouflage it for the screen, but Melissa thought that was a mistake. The small imperfection made him more human. She had an almost irresistible urge to reach out and touch it.

"I don't accept rejection easily," he warned. "It would save a lot of time if you gave in now."

Melissa glanced automatically at her watch, then drew in her breath sharply. "I have to go! I'm going to be late."

"For what?"

She put the car in drive. "I'll be here on Friday."

Granger's eyes were narrowed in thought as he watched Melissa barrel down the driveway.

Chapter Three

Granger continued to be persistent in the days that followed. Although Melissa turned down all of his invitations, he kept asking her to have dinner with him. She was convinced that it was merely reflex action by now, but she couldn't help enjoying his company. When Granger wasn't being too inquisitive, he was a fascinating companion.

After that one lapse of judgment, Melissa refused to go swimming again, but Granger helped her in the garden and kept her amused with stories about the rich and famous. Melissa looked forward more and more to the days she spent at his house, especially since she knew that Granger wouldn't be part of them for long.

At the end of her second week there he asked, "Do you have a big weekend planned?"

"More or less." Melissa braced herself for an invitation he didn't extend.

Granger was lying on the grass with his arms crossed behind his head. He stared up at the clear blue sky. "Maybe I'll take a run up to Lake Arrowhead. I'm getting tired of hanging around doing nothing."

Melissa had seen this coming, but she still felt a pang. Some of the color would go out of her life when *he* did.

"The weather might still be a little cool at night in the mountains," she commented.

"I like it crisp. There's nothing like lying in front of a crackling fire with a hot toddy."

And a compliant female. Melissa silently supplied the small detail he omitted. She glanced away, trying not to picture that hard, rangy body holding a softer form in his arms.

"Too bad it's seldom cold enough in Los Angeles for a fire in the fireplace," she remarked.

"Well, you can't have everything."

Granger's words lingered in Melissa's ears as she drove home that afternoon. With a few casual words he'd summed up her life. Outside of Betsy what did she have? Melissa pushed the thought away impatiently. She didn't *need* anyone but her daughter.

The doorbell rang about six o'clock that evening. Melissa was in the kitchen making coleslaw to go with the hot dogs and baked beans that were Betsy's favorite meal.

"Will you answer that, honey?" Melissa called to her daughter. "But be sure you ask who it is before you open the door."

"Okay." The little girl went to the door and did as she'd been told.

"It's Granger McMasters," a voice outside answered.

"Are you the man my mother works for?" she called through the door.

A look of surprise crossed his face. "Your mother?"

"Uh-huh. She works for a big movie star. Is that you?"

"I guess it must be. May I speak to her?"

"Sure." Betsy opened the door and looked with frank curiosity at the tall man standing on the doorstep. "Hi, I'm Betsy. I never met a movie star before."

He regarded her with equal interest. "We're not very different from normal people."

"Mom says you live in a different world."

Granger lifted one eyebrow. "So does your mother— a cloistered one."

"What does that mean?"

"It was merely an opinion." He glanced around the small living room. "Is your father home yet? I'd like to meet him."

"I don't have a father. I did when I was a baby, but he had to go away."

"I'm sorry," Granger said gently.

"It would be nice to have a father, but Mom and I have fun together."

"I'm sure you do. Your mother is a lovely lady."

"She takes me lots of places, but we can't afford to go to Hawaii," Betsy said matter-of-factly.

Granger cleared his throat. "Maybe you will one day."

Melissa had paused until she heard Betsy talking to someone, then resumed chopping cabbage. It was probably Vivian on her way home from work, she decided. Their voices were indistinct because of the newscast on TV.

But when Betsy didn't return after a few moments, Melissa went to investigate. Her eyes widened when she saw Granger standing by the front door.

"What are you doing here?" she gasped.

"I had a glib excuse prepared, but now I feel a little foolish," he said. "You have a lovely daughter."

"Thank you," Melissa answered stiffly. Her voice softened when she said, "Betsy, dear, run in the kitchen and stir the beans for me, will you?"

When the little girl left the room, Granger said, "She's a beautiful child."

Melissa ignored that. "How did you know where to find me?"

"Bill has your address and phone number on file."

"So you decided to see how the other half lives." She waved her arm around the apartment.

Granger gazed at her steadily. "If you believe that, then I did make a mistake in coming here."

"I'm sorry," she mumbled.

Melissa knew she'd been unfair, but seeing him here in her home was unsettling. It was as though Granger were stripping away her defenses one by one.

Betsy returned. "I stirred the beans," she announced. "Is Mr. McMasters staying for dinner?"

"No, he has another engagement," Melissa answered swiftly.

"Actually, it fell through," he said smoothly. "I'd be happy to stay, if I were invited."

"Oh, goody! We hardly ever have company," Betsy said. "I'll go set another place at the table."

"Why are you doing this?" Melissa asked plaintively. "You can't really want to have dinner with a seven-year-old."

His expression was unreadable as he gazed at her troubled face. "You don't know anything about me, in spite of all the time we've spent together these past two weeks."

"Most of that time you spent asking me about myself."

"Tonight I'm going to get some answers. Can we have a drink before dinner?"

"I'm afraid I don't have anything except some cooking sherry and a little crème de menthe."

Granger made a face. "Hold dinner, I'll be right back. Betsy," he called. "Do you want to go to the market with me and pick out something for dessert?"

"That isn't necessary," Melissa said. "I have cookies."

"Does that compare to chocolate élairs?" he asked Betsy.

"No way." She grinned.

Melissa had definite misgivings as she watched Betsy put her small hand trustingly in Granger's large one. She looked so happy. More than a chocolate éclair warranted. Did Betsy miss having a father? Melissa had tried hard to fill the gap, and Betsy was so well adjusted that she thought she'd succeeded. But Granger was leading her daughter away like the pied piper of Hamelin. Was it his intention to take over her own life completely?

Melissa suddenly realized she didn't have time for introspection. Before Granger returned she needed to change clothes. After work she usually changed into a clean pair of jeans and a cotton shirt. But wouldn't you know it? Today she'd chosen a thin caftan, with only a pair of panties underneath.

The black turtleneck jersey and tailored pants she hurriedly pulled on made her feel better. Then she brushed her hair and applied light coral lipstick and a touch of mascara. Not to make herself more attractive for Granger, Melissa assured herself, simply to look presentable.

Granger had a large grocery bag in his arms, and Betsy was carrying a square bakery box when they returned.

"We got chocolate éclairs and cream puffs, too," she announced.

"Whose idea was that?" Melissa teased.

"I got to choose," Betsy admitted.

"That's an awfully big bag. What's in it?" Melissa asked Granger as she followed him to the kitchen.

"Scotch, bourbon, gin and vodka." He began unloading bottles on the counter. "I forgot to ask what you drink."

"Very little," she answered. "What am I going to do with all of that?"

"You'll be prepared the next time you have a thirsty gentleman caller. I also got a bottle of wine for dinner."

"I hope it's an unpretentious little vintage that goes with frankfurters and beans. That's what we're having." Melissa got out two highball glasses and filled an ice bucket from the freezer.

"Great. I haven't had franks and beans in a long time," he said.

"Why doesn't that surprise me?" she asked dryly, nodding as he held up the bottle of Scotch with a questioning expression.

"You're still convinced that I dine on filet mignon and broiled lobster every night."

"Maybe not, but I'll bet you don't eat in the kitchen."

"I would if I had two beautiful blondes to share it with me." He smiled at Betsy.

"Do you have any little girls?" she asked.

"No, but I hope to some day."

"Do you have a wife?" Betsy persisted.

"Not yet."

"You have to have a wife before you can have babies," she told him.

Granger looked at Melissa with suppressed amusement. "Did she learn the facts of life from you?"

"Go wash your hands for dinner," she told her daughter hastily.

Betsy provided the buffer that allowed Melissa to enjoy herself. Granger was always exciting to be around, even when he was being difficult. But with a child present, he had to be on his good behavior. Betsy was entranced with him, and he seemed intrigued by her, too. Melissa was skeptical at first, but his interest didn't appear to be forced. Granger seemed to genuinely like children.

"Mom says you have a swimming pool in your backyard," Betsy remarked during dinner.

"Do you like to swim?" he asked.

"Oh, yes. Sometimes we go to the beach, but I don't get to swim in a swimming pool very often," she commented ingenuously.

"You can use mine anytime you like."

"Tomorrow?"

"It isn't polite to invite yourself to someone's house," Melissa said reprovingly.

"But how would he know when I wanted to come if I didn't tell him?" Betsy complained.

Granger chuckled. "I like directness in a female. It's so rare."

"Does that mean we can come?" Betsy asked.

"Unless you'd rather go to Disneyland," he answered. "Your mother sees enough of my place during the week."

"Do you really mean it?" The little girl's face was filled with rapture. "I've never been to Disneyland."

"You're joking!" He looked at Melissa disapprovingly. "You've never taken her to Disneyland?"

She pushed the last of her éclair around the plate. "It's a little exhausting for a small child."

"I'm seven!" Betsy said indignantly.

Melissa was caught in an awkward situation. The famous amusement park was a costly day's outing. The entrance fee was high, although it included unlimited rides—but not parking. There was also lunch to buy and snacks, plus the souvenirs that children pined after. Granger couldn't conceive of not having an extra fifty or sixty dollars to spend, and Melissa wasn't going to enlighten him. She certainly didn't want his pity.

"Almost all the kids in my class have been there." Betsy pursued her grievance at being considered too young.

"Tomorrow you're going to join their ranks," Granger assured her.

"Can we, Mom? Can we?" Betsy beseeched her.

How could she say no? "If Mr. McMasters is really serious," Melissa answered slowly.

"I'm looking forward to it," he replied.

"Wow! Wait till I tell Cathy. She's my best friend," Betsy informed Granger.

"Would you like to ask her to join us?" he asked.

"Could I?" she asked breathlessly.

"Sure. Let's decide when we want to leave."

After they'd settled on the time and Betsy had gone to phone Cathy, Melissa looked at Granger in bewilderment. "I don't understand you at all."

"I've been telling you that for two weeks. What specifically don't you understand?"

"You told me yourself that you can't do the things normal people do."

"Is that what's bothering you? Let me worry about it."

"You know what will happen when people recognize you. You'll be mobbed for autographs."

"It's better than being ignored." He grinned.

"Get real, Granger! You're going to hate it."

"Wait and see." He rose and picked up the dessert plates. "Let's wash the dishes."

"Just put them on the sink. I'll do them after you leave."

"If that's a hint, I'm not taking it." He removed his jacket and rolled up his shirtsleeves.

"You'll get your clothes dirty," Melissa warned.

"Cleaners have to make a living, too. You can put away the leftovers while I load the dishwasher."

"At least let me give you an apron."

The floral apron she draped around him didn't diminish Granger's virility in the slightest. Nor did it make him self-conscious. Granger might have been any normal husband helping his wife with the dishes—if ordinary husbands wore Brioni slacks and custom-made silk shirts.

"You're a handy man to have around," she remarked lightly.

"You sound surprised. Didn't your husband help out in the kitchen?"

"He said that was women's work."

Granger lifted an eyebrow. "What's men's work?"

"Something more recreational," she answered briefly.

Before he could comment, Betsy returned with the news that Cathy could go with them the next day. The little girl was so excited over the coming event that she couldn't stop talking about it from then on. And when it was time for bed, she didn't even plead to stay up later the way she normally did on the weekend.

After Melissa had tucked Betsy in and rejoined Granger in the living room, she commented on the fact. "It isn't usually this easy to get her to go to sleep. She always has a long list of reasons why she's old enough to stay up later."

"That's standard procedure. The early cave children probably deviled their parents the same way," Granger said.

"I wonder what excuse they used before television was invented."

"That's easy." He chuckled. "Og gets to stay up later. Why can't I?"

"How do you know so much about children?" she asked curiously.

"I was a seven-year-old once."

That was hard to believe. Granger was unmistakably grown-up now. As she gazed at his long-limbed frame relaxed on the couch, Melissa felt her nerves tighten. She was self-conscious with him now that they were alone together.

Granger wasn't similarly affected. He patted the cushion beside him. "Sit down and relax. You've had a full day."

"No busier than usual."

Melissa sat at the other end of the couch, which wasn't that far from Granger since it was a small couch. She would have preferred a chair, but she didn't want him to know his proximity disturbed her.

"Working every day and caring for a youngster can't be easy," he remarked.

"I'm luckier than a lot of women. I can arrange my hours so I'm home when Betsy gets out of school."

"At last I found out what the big rush was to leave my place."

"Now you know all my secrets," Melissa said jokingly.

"Not all of them. What happened to your husband? Betsy said he had to go away?"

Melissa's long lashes swept down. "I'd prefer not to talk about it."

"I'm sorry," Granger said gently. "Betsy spoke of him so unemotionally. I didn't know the loss was recent."

"Stan left years ago, and he wasn't any loss," Melissa said bluntly.

Granger stared at her in surprise. "I gathered he was dead."

"Not as far as I know, but you couldn't prove it by me."

"You'd know if his checks stopped coming."

"What checks?" Melissa asked derisively.

"Surely you were awarded child support."

"*Awarded* is one thing, collecting is something else."

Granger frowned. "A man is responsible for the children he fathers."

"Let's just say he should be. You'd be surprised at the number of men who simply drop out of sight to avoid paying."

"That means giving up their children. Doesn't he ever come to see Betsy?"

"She's never even gotten a birthday card from him."

"How do you explain that to a seven-year-old?"

Melissa's lip curled. "It's easy to buy a present and sign his name. I did that even when he was around."

"Doesn't she ever want to know why he never comes home?"

"She did in the beginning, but children have short memories. Betsy was only four when Stan left. She barely remembers him."

"Even so, she's bound to ask questions when she gets older."

"I suppose she will someday, as a matter of curiosity. It's not a problem now. At the present moment Betsy is more concerned about having a stepfather." Melissa smiled wryly. "At least I could set her mind at rest on that point."

Granger's eyes wandered over her delicate features. "You don't ever expect to remarry?"

"I don't have very good judgment when it comes to men."

"Because you made one mistake? You can't let that ruin your entire life."

"I like my life just fine the way it is. I can do what I want, when I want, without having to answer to anyone."

"That's nice, but is it enough to forgo love?"

She flicked an invisible piece of lint off her knee. "I'm not sure I know what the word means. I thought I loved Stan."

"All right then, how about companionship?"

"I have Betsy."

"I'm talking about male companionship."

"You mean sex," she answered scornfully.

"No, I was referring to caring and togetherness, someone to share with. When you've had a bad day, as we all do on occasion, haven't you ever wanted to curl up in someone's arms and tell him about it?"

"Men aren't interested in talking, especially under the circumstances you're describing."

"Poor Melissa. You've never met a real man."

Granger's throaty voice sent a shiver down her spine. She jumped up from the couch. "You're wasting your pity on the wrong person."

He rose, also, and put his hands on her rigid shoulders. "You're confusing pity with sympathy. You picked a real jerk, and I'm sorry you got hurt."

"I got over it a long time ago," she mumbled.

"I don't think so." His hands moved to circle her neck. They felt warm and strong. "You need somebody to tell you how desirable you are. I don't think you realize what an exquisite woman you are."

Melissa's legs felt like rubber bands. She tried to look amused, to cover up her terrible vulnerability to him. If Granger took her in his arms, she was afraid she wouldn't resist.

"Is that your good deed for today? Convincing a jilted wife that she's still attractive to men?" Her laughter sounded forced in spite of her efforts.

"You are to me." His fingers trailed down her cheek to trace the contours of her trembling mouth. "I'd like to make love to you the way you deserve, with infinite time to discover the things that please you."

She was mesmerized by his sensuous caress and the light in his gray eyes. Melissa dug her nails into her palms to break his spell. "What happened to companionship?"

He chuckled softly. "I promise we'd be very close."

She forced herself to move away. "I'm not looking for that kind of closeness."

"Don't knock it until you've tried it," he teased.

She shook her head. "I'm sure you have a proven track record, but you'll have to chalk tonight up as one of your few failures."

He looked amused. "Contrary to what you think, all my evenings don't wind up in bed—at least not with company. I didn't expect this one would, if you want the truth."

"It was different for you, anyway," she said brightly. "Where are you going from here?"

"Home. We have a strenuous day ahead of us."

"I hope you know what you're letting yourself in for. Two little girls will be a handful. I have trouble keeping track of *one*."

"But tomorrow you'll have someone to share the responsibility." He smiled winningly.

"You have an idealized view of children," she warned.

"I'm a realist," he answered. "I know exactly what to expect. You're the one who's due for a surprise."

"You'd better get a good night's sleep just to be on the safe side."

"You don't leave me any alternative." He laughed. "Thanks for a nice dinner and an enjoyable evening."

Melissa walked him to the door with a mixture of relief and regret. She'd resisted him successfully, but Granger would be an experience no woman would ever forget, she thought wistfully.

He took both of her hands in his. "I'll see you tomorrow morning at ten." Lowering his head, he kissed her cheek.

Melissa stared at the closed door after he had gone. She felt let down and keyed up at the same time, as though something was unfinished between them. Maybe it was his good-night kiss. She could scarcely object to such a fleeting caress on the cheek, but her skin glowed where his lips had touched it. What if he'd kissed her on the mouth?

Melissa hurriedly turned out the lights and went to bed.

Betsy was up even earlier than usual the next morning. She always let Melissa sleep later on Saturdays, but today she tiptoed into the bedroom half a dozen times and stood over the bed, sighing audibly. Finally Melissa gave up and opened her eyes.

"I didn't mean to wake you," Betsy said anxiously. "I just came in to see if you were up."

"I am now." Melissa laughed, pulling the little girl into her arms.

"We have to hurry." Betsy struggled to her feet. "Mr. McMasters will be here soon."

"Not for three hours."

"You don't think he'll forget, do you?" The child's eyes darkened with worry.

"I know he won't," Melissa assured her.

"He's a nice man. I like him."

"Most females do." Melissa got out of bed and put on her robe.

Betsy's smooth brow wrinkled. "Don't you like Mr. McMasters, Mom?"

"Of course I do," Melissa answered swiftly. "Give me a few minutes to shower, and I'll fix breakfast."

Their early start made the morning seem endless. Melissa was thankful when Cathy arrived, so Betsy would stop dogging her footsteps and let her straighten up the house. She gave immediate permission when the little girls asked if they could sit on the front steps to wait for Granger.

"I've never been so glad to see anybody in my life," Melissa told him when he finally arrived.

"Maybe I went home too early last night," Granger murmured.

She gave him a reproving look. "The girls have been driving me crazy."

"They have that effect on me, too, when they get older." He smiled.

Betsy tugged on his sleeve, impatient with adult repartee. "Can we go now?"

The children were entranced with Disneyland. They had their picture taken with Donald Duck, rode down Main Street in a horse-drawn surrey and stood in line for all the rides. Melissa and Granger trailed along behind, marveling at their energy.

"They're going to crash when they get home tonight," he observed.

"You should feel really good about making two little girls this happy," Melissa told him.

"It's a privilege." He put his arm around her shoulders and gave her an affectionate squeeze. "I'd like to make a big girl happy, too."

"I'm not that easy." She smiled up at him, feeling happiness flood through her veins. "You'll have to buy me popcorn first."

"With extra butter," he promised.

Granger had his mouth full when an older couple approached them. The woman stared at him avidly.

"Aren't you Granger McMasters?" she asked breathlessly.

He chuckled. "People are always asking me that. The missus gets a big kick out of it, don't you, hon?"

Melissa looked at him critically. "Personally, I don't see the resemblance at all."

The woman gazed at Granger's handsome face and splendid physique, not fully convinced that she'd made a mistake. "You're sure you're not him?"

"I told you he couldn't be," her husband said. "What would a big movie star be doing here, walking around like everybody else? You'll have to excuse my wife," he said to Granger. "Helen's crazy about celebrities."

"Sorry to disappoint her," Granger smiled.

"My husband is kind of a celebrity in Klamath Falls where we come from," Melissa said demurely. "He's the local sheriff up there."

"Maybe you should get his autograph, Helen," the man joked, leading her away.

"Well, he *looked* like him," she insisted.

"Poor thing," Melissa said. "He'll never let her hear the end of it."

"That was a nice touch you added," Granger said approvingly. "I think I'll buy a tin badge and keep it in my pocket for authenticity."

The incident was amusing until it was repeated several times. Granger's disclaimer was always met with incredulity, then questions about whether he'd ever thought of doubling for the famous star. This often led to stories about friends or relatives of theirs who were also dead ringers for some celebrity or other. The game wore thin after a while.

"It might be easier just to sign autographs," Melissa commented when the latest fans had left.

"I have a better solution." Granger took her hand and led her behind a building. "Do you have a mirror in your purse?" he asked.

She produced a small one. "Will this do?"

"Perfect. Hold it up for me."

As Melissa watched curiously, Granger took a fake mustache out of his pocket and stuck it on his upper lip. Then he put on a pair of wire-rimmed glasses and a fisherman's cap. The transformation was startling. He was still an attractive man, but not as overwhelmingly so.

"I don't think we'll be bothered anymore," he said with satisfaction.

"I'd bet on it! You look completely different." She reached out to touch his mustache. "Can you talk and eat and everything without having it fall off?"

"I'm not sure about the everything part. It might not be kissproof," he teased. "Shall we test it and find out?"

"That won't be necessary. The occasion isn't apt to arise."

"You never can tell."

He cupped her face in his palms and kissed her lightly. The whole incident might have passed as a joke, but Melissa's lips parted, completely against her will. Granger reacted immediately. Gathering her in his arms, he molded her body to his while he deepened the kiss.

Melissa clung to him for a mindless moment, conscious only of his hard angles and firm mouth. They were powerfully seductive, making any resistance unthinkable. Tiny sparks shot through her, ignited by the warmth of his body.

"My sweet Melissa." Granger buried his face in her hair. "I've wanted to do that for weeks."

Sanity returned, and she was appalled at her weakness. Putting distance between them, Melissa stared at his mustache, avoiding his eyes. "It's still there. I guess you have nothing to worry about."

"Neither do you," he answered gently. "Don't be afraid of me, honey. I'll never hurt you."

Perhaps not on purpose. All the evidence showed that Granger was a decent man, but he held a compelling attraction for her. There was no use denying it. She could easily fall in love with him, and then what? They came from different worlds and wanted different things from a relationship.

"We'd better get back," she said in a muted voice. "The riverboat ride will be over soon, and the girls will be looking for us."

"Whatever you say," he answered quietly.

The girls went into a fit of giggles when they saw Granger. "You look so funny," Cathy chortled.

"I thought I looked rather dashing." He stroked the fake lip adornment.

"Where did you get it?" Betsy asked.

"In one of the shops. Would you like one?"

"Girls don't wear mustaches," she protested, laughing.

"They can do anything they want." He gazed at Melissa. "All they have to do is get rid of their inhibitions."

"I'd rather have Mickey Mouse ears. Can we, Mr. McMasters?"

"You mustn't ask for things," Melissa chided automatically. She was very conscious of Granger's steady gaze.

"She was only expressing a preference," he said. "Come on, let's go shopping."

The little girls wanted everything they saw in the gift store, and Granger bought it for them, over Melissa's objections. After the children were loaded down with toys and souvenirs, he suggested ice cream.

They found a restaurant with a large outdoor patio. When they were seated at a table, Granger allowed them to order whatever they wanted from the extensive menu.

"You're spoiling them dreadfully," Melissa said.

"One day of wild excess won't leave a permanent mark." He smiled.

"As long as they realize that fairy godfathers don't turn up with any regularity," she answered.

"I never heard of fairy godfathers," Cathy said. "Cinderella had a fairy god*mother*."

"They didn't have equal opportunity in those days," Granger told her.

When Cathy looked puzzled, Melissa said wryly, "Mr. McMasters is only teasing you. He does that to girls sometimes."

"That's what you choose to believe." Granger covered Melissa's hand on the table.

"I think they like each other." Cathy's stage whisper to Betsy was audible.

"Eat your ice cream before it melts," Melissa told her, more sharply than she meant to.

Betsy was looking speculatively at Granger. "Can I call you Uncle Granger?"

"No." His smiled was replaced by a slight frown.

Melissa guessed the reason for his refusal. Children often referred to their mother's lovers as "Uncle." Melissa was touched by Granger's sensitivity.

"You're a very nice man," she said softly.

"I try." He turned back to Betsy, who was looking rebuffed. "Why don't you call me Mac? That's what my good friends call me."

Her little face cleared. "I like that name."

The afternoon passed all too swiftly for the girls. They didn't want to leave, but in the car on the way home, they had trouble keeping their eyes open.

"I'll bet you won't get any arguments at bedtime," Granger remarked.

"They had a wonderful day. One they won't forget for a long time."

"How about you? Was today the ordeal you expected?"

Her eyes widened. "How did you know?"

"It figures. You don't want to let any man close to you, and I have a tendency to break the rules."

Her laughter was shaky. "At least you admit it."

"That's the only way I can get through the wall you've built around yourself."

"You're wrong about me. I don't hate all men. As a matter of fact, you've changed my views considerably."

"That's encouraging. How did I do that?"

"Well, you're kind and thoughtful and generous."

"I didn't hear charming or sexy," he teased.

"There are children present." Melissa glanced at the back seat, but the girls weren't paying any attention to them.

"We'll discuss the subject further over dinner tonight when they're not around. Where would you like to go?"

"I can't leave Betsy."

"Of course you can. Call a sitter."

"I don't know any sitters."

Granger raised an eyebrow. "You never go out without her?"

"Not very often. Once in a while a friend who's a nurse comes over to baby-sit, but she's on night duty this week."

"Then call an agency," he said with dwindling patience.

"I couldn't leave Betsy with a stranger."

"Those women are thoroughly checked out, and she isn't a helpless infant. Aren't you being overly protective?"

Melissa was unwilling to explain to Granger that she couldn't afford the rates an agency charged. He would offer to pay, and she didn't want him to. That wasn't the normal obligation of a date. Foolish or not, it would make her feel like a charity case.

"We've had such a lovely day, Granger. Why don't we just leave it at that? I'm really rather tired myself."

He shrugged. "If that's the way you want it."

Although he was pleasant during the rest of the trip home, Melissa knew that Granger was displeased with her. He dropped Cathy off at her house and walked Betsy and Melissa to the front door of their apartment, but he didn't come in.

Betsy hugged him in an excess of gratitude, and he hugged her in return, seeming pleased. His leave-taking from Melissa was more restrained.

"Thanks again for everything," she said.

"It was my pleasure," he answered politely. "Get some rest. You do look tired."

Melissa should have been happy. She'd effectively discouraged Granger. Her eyes were wistful, though, as she watched his car drive away—for the last time.

Chapter Four

Betsy slept late the next morning after her strenuous day, but Melissa was up early, in spite of a restless night. She couldn't stop thinking about Granger. He'd never been that cool toward her. Would he ask her out again? And if he did, should she accept?

For once, Betsy was no help as a distraction. When she awoke later in the morning, the little girl couldn't stop talking about the previous day. Naturally Granger's name came up repeatedly.

"Mac looked so funny in that mustache," Betsy said with a giggle during breakfast. "I'll bet it tickled."

If it had, Melissa wasn't aware of it. Her pulse quickened as she remembered Granger's soul-stirring kiss. He'd felt the magic, too. Or was it merely desire on his part? That was more likely.

"You're not listening to me," Betsy complained. "I asked if we could go swimming at Mac's today."

"No. He spent all day yesterday with us. We can't take advantage of his good nature."

"He *said* we could come anytime we wanted."

"Not today. Weren't you going to phone Cathy about something?" Melissa asked to distract her.

Betsy went over to Cathy's house to play, leaving Melissa with a free afternoon. That was usually a luxury, yet she felt restless and keyed up. Was this the end of her friendship with Granger? Maybe he would phone to show her there were no hard feelings.

But the day dragged by and the evening, too, without a word from him.

Melissa went to Granger's house on Monday morning, uncertain about how to handle the situation. She needn't have worried. He wasn't at home, nor did he appear all afternoon. The same was true of Wednesday.

By Friday she was forced to accept the fact that Granger had written her off. It was disappointing to find out he was like all other men—interested in only one thing. Melissa tried to tell herself she was lucky to have found that out before their friendship turned into anything else on her part. But she didn't feel lucky. Underneath her disillusion was a deep sense of loss.

That Saturday night Betsy had gone to take a bath before getting into bed. As Melissa was looking at the television listings, the doorbell rang.

When she opened the door, Granger greeted her as though nothing had happened between them. "Hi, I hope this isn't too late to drop in."

Melissa couldn't speak for a moment. The unexpected sight of him brought a surge of happiness that was disconcerting. Granger was even more virile than usual in a gray leather jacket and oxford-gray slacks. He looked rugged and fit and extremely masculine.

His smile faded when she continued to stare at him silently. "Have I come at a bad time?" He glanced over her shoulder.

"No, not at all! Come in. I . . . I was just surprised to see you. You haven't been around much lately."

"I had to go to New York unexpectedly. Didn't Mrs. Flannery tell you?"

"No. I suppose she didn't think it concerned me," Melissa said ruefully.

Granger made a sound of annoyance. "I told her to tell you where I'd gone."

"We were both busy. She and I never get a chance to talk much." Melissa didn't see what would be gained by getting the woman in trouble. "Did you have a nice time?"

"It was a business trip, but I did manage to see a couple of shows."

"I envy you. New York is such an exciting city," she commented.

"There's no place like it," he agreed.

Betsy came into the living room in a bathrobe and slippers. Her face lit up when she saw Granger. "Mom didn't tell me you were coming!" she exclaimed.

"She didn't know," he answered. "I just dropped by."

"Cathy and I had a really neat time at Disneyland last week," Betsy said enthusiastically. "We told everybody at school about it."

"I had a neat time, too," Granger answered fondly.

"Some of the kids didn't believe you really took us."

"Why didn't you show them your Mickey Mouse ears?"

"Oh, they know we went to Disneyland. They just don't believe we went with *you*. They said a big movie star wouldn't waste time with little kids like us."

"People have a lot of misconceptions about so-called stars." Granger glanced at Melissa. "There's not a lot you can do about it."

"You changed *my* mind," she said softly.

"That's good news." Something kindled in the depths of his gray eyes.

Betsy didn't want his attention to slip away. "Did you really mean it when you said we could swim in your pool? Mom keeps saying we can't."

Granger looked at Melissa with amusement. "Haven't you heard that the third time's a charm?"

Her cheeks warmed as she remembered her two previous mishaps. "I suppose nothing worse could happen."

"That depends on your definition of worse," he murmured. "I thoroughly enjoyed myself."

"Mom says we have to wait for an invitation." Betsy guided him back to the subject.

"Your mother is a very proper lady," he teased. "She doesn't believe in getting too familiar."

"Would you like some coffee?" Melissa asked hurriedly.

"If it's not too much trouble," he answered politely, stifling his laughter as he followed her into the kitchen.

Betsy tagged along. "Can I have some cookies and milk?"

"It's past your bedtime," Melissa said doubtfully.

"Tomorrow's Sunday. I don't have to get up early," the little girl coaxed.

"All right, you can stay up for half an hour."

"I wish *I* could talk your mother into things that easily." Granger chuckled.

"You do, repeatedly," Melissa said dryly.

"Nothing you don't really want to do." His eyes held hers.

Betsy tugged at his sleeve. "My friend Tiffany says if I really knew you, I'd bring your autograph to school to show everybody."

"That's no problem," Granger said. "What if I gave you a signed picture? Would that do it?"

"Oh, yes! Could you bring it tomorrow? I want to take it to school on Monday. That Tiffany thinks she's so smart." The little girl's voice held resentment. "She acts like she knows everything just because she played spin the bottle at a party once."

"At seven years old?" Melissa gasped.

"Kids are getting more sophisticated all the time," Granger commented.

"Tiffany says she likes kissing boys," Betsy announced.

"I imagine they enjoyed it, too." He grinned. "She sounds very precocious."

"Will *I* like it?" Betsy asked.

"I'm sure you will—when you get older," Granger added after a look at Melissa's face.

"A lot of girls in the fifth grade have boyfriends," Betsy remarked thoughtfully.

Melissa frowned. "Mac meant a lot older than that."

"Did you have a girlfriend when you were young?" Betsy asked him.

He laughed. "Not when I was as young as you are."

"I'll bet!" Melissa muttered under her breath.

Granger gave her an amused glance. "In spite of what your mother believes, I was more interested in sports when I was in grade school."

"I like baseball, but the boys won't ever let the girls play with them," Betsy complained.

"That's because they'd never live it down if you got more hits than they did. Boys have very fragile egos."

"You mean, they have to be best at everything?"

Granger smiled. "They like to think they are, but a smart woman can get the better of a man anyday."

"That's a lovely fairy tale," Melissa observed tartly. "It's time for bed," she told Betsy.

"Can't I stay up a little bit longer?"

"You already did. Say good-night to Mac."

"Okay." Betsy put her arms around his neck and kissed his cheek.

He held her close for a moment. "Sleep tight, little one," he said in a husky voice.

Melissa looked troubled when she returned from tucking Betsy in. "I don't know what got into that child tonight. All that talk about kissing. She's never had the slightest interest in boys before."

"Are you sure?" Granger asked. "Maybe she didn't bring up the subject because she knows how you feel about the opposite sex."

"That's ridiculous! I've certainly never discussed my feelings with her. Are you saying I'm warping my daughter?" Melissa demanded heatedly.

"Relax, honey. I'm not criticizing you. The answer is a lot less complicated than that. Betsy has never had a man in her life. She feels comfortable with me, so she took this opportunity to get a male point of view on a lot of things she's been curious about."

"You don't have to remind me that Betsy doesn't have a father," Melissa said slowly. "I worry about it constantly, but what can I do?"

"You're doing just fine," he soothed. "She's an adorable, well-adjusted child."

"I thought so, but now I'm not so sure. I guess it was unrealistic to think I could be enough for her."

"Stop blaming yourself for something you had no control over. The guy who ran out on you is the one who's at fault. You've done a great job without him."

"I've tried to do my best, but the problem is only going to get worse." Melissa sighed. "There will be lots of times when Betsy will need a father's advice."

"Perhaps you should let a man into your life," Granger said casually.

"I'd do anything in the world for my daughter, but I don't think marrying the first man who asks me is the solution. He might not turn out any better than her real father."

"I wasn't suggesting anything that drastic."

"What else is there?"

"Men and women can be friends. You and I are. Why not let me help out when you think Betsy needs male guidance?"

"I couldn't ask you to do that. We barely know each other."

"I disagree. We've shared quite a few experiences." He smiled. "But in any case, friendship isn't based on the length of time you've known someone, it's how you feel about a person. Doesn't that make sense?"

"Well, yes," she faltered.

"Maybe you have some other objections. Do you think I'd be a bad influence on Betsy?"

"No, I think you're a very kind man," Melissa said softly.

"Within limits." He grinned. "I'd still like to make love to you, but I won't let that affect my relationship with your daughter."

"I'm glad we're not a package deal," Melissa said lightly.

"It's your loss," he joked. "You're missing a bet by turning down all my invitations."

"I didn't know you'd give up so easily," she murmured.

"Don't you believe it. I'm a fool for lost causes. Just to show you, I'll ask again. Will you have dinner with me tomorrow night?"

"I'd love to," she answered promptly.

Instead of looking pleased, he gazed at her impassively. "Is that my reward for offering to be helpful? Because if it is, you don't have to make the sacrifice. There were no strings attached to my offer."

"I know that."

"They why the sudden change of heart?"

"I like being with you," she answered honestly. "When I thought I wouldn't see you anymore, I missed you."

"That's very sweet," he said huskily.

She smiled wryly at him. "Women aren't supposed to say that to men, but I'm not very good at playing games."

He took both of her hands in his big strong ones. "Don't ever change. You're a very rare lady."

Granger's touch and the brilliance in his eyes made her feel like warm taffy, soft and yielding. Melissa was achingly aware of how quiet the apartment was.

She jumped up and went over to turn on the stove. "I'll heat up the coffee."

"Not for me, thanks." Granger stood and stretched, as relaxed as Melissa was taut. "I'd better go home and get a good night's sleep. I have a big evening coming up." He grinned mischievously.

"What time does this big evening start?" she asked casually.

"I'll pick you up at eight. Is that all right?"

"Perfect."

"That's what *I* think." He tilted her chin up and kissed her lightly.

It was a brief caress. Nothing she could object to—or consider significant. She was careful not to react.

After Granger left, Melissa rinsed their cups and went into the living room to watch television. She couldn't concentrate, though. Excitement coursed through her veins like bubbling champagne.

"Anyone would think you'd never had a date," she muttered disgustedly. But it *had* been a long time. And never with a man like Granger.

"Do I look all right?" Melissa stared at herself in the mirror the next night.

"You look smashing," Vivian assured her. "You can't go wrong with a little black dress."

"It's kind of plain," Melissa answered dubiously.

Her concern was misplaced. The dress was unadorned, but it clung to her slender figure in all the right places, and accentuated her fair skin.

"You just need some jewelry to jazz it up a bit."

"I don't have anything very dramatic."

"That's what I figured, so I brought these." Vivian delved into her large purse and brought out a pair of long, dangling rhinestone earrings, and a chunky bracelet that looked enough like gold to be the real thing.

Melissa fastened the earrings to her lobes and inspected herself with a slight frown. "I don't want to sound ungrateful, but aren't they a bit much?"

"Get with it. These are the latest thing." Vivian clasped the bracelet around Melissa's wrist and stepped back to view the result. "See? Doesn't that make a difference?"

"It does brighten it up somewhat. Not that anything could make this old dress look like haute couture."

"Don't be too sure. The simpler an outfit is, the more expensive it looks."

Melissa gathered her long hair in both hands. "Maybe I should tie my hair back so the earrings show better."

"No, don't. It's sexier to see them peeking out when you turn your head."

"I'm not trying to look sexy."

"Well, you should be. Think of all the glamorous women you're up against."

"I couldn't possibly compete," Melissa answered hopelessly.

"Don't you ever look in the mirror?"

Vivian gazed at her friend admiringly. Melissa's slim figure and long legs were the equal of any high-fashion model, and her face could have graced a magazine cover.

"Granger is used to women who have exciting careers." Melissa sighed. "They know all the in places and new trends. What do I have to talk about?"

"You spent a whole day with him and you didn't have any trouble."

"That was different. The girls were there."

"You mean, he couldn't very well make a pass at you," Vivian said shrewdly. "That's what's really bothering you, isn't it?"

"Maybe," Melissa admitted. "I really like being with Granger. I don't want anything to spoil our relationship."

"I'd say that would cement it."

"For how long? I'm not interested in a brief fling."

Vivian gave her a troubled look. "What *do* you want? You're not falling in love with him, are you?"

"No, of course not," Melissa answered swiftly. "He's simply a good friend that I wouldn't want to lose."

"Then enjoy, for heaven's sake! And if that includes making out a little—well, enjoy that, too." Vivian grinned.

The doorbell rang before Melissa could reply. She sent Vivian to answer it, partly to compose herself and partly to reward her friend with a few moments alone with Granger.

When she joined them in the living room, Vivian had a dazzled expression on her face. Melissa didn't blame her. She'd never seen Granger in a suit and tie before, and the sight was impressive. His broad shoulders were emphasized by the perfectly draped jacket, and the snowy linen showing at the cuffs and neck contrasted with his deep tan.

"How lovely you look." His gaze wandered from Melissa's finely chiseled features to the honey-colored hair curling around her slim shoulders.

"You do, too," she blurted out.

Granger laughed. "No one's ever called me lovely before. At least, not to my knowledge."

Really sophisticated, Melissa chastised herself disgustedly. "I meant, you look very dashing."

"That's nice." He smiled. "Where's Betsy? I'd like to say hello to her before we leave."

"She's in bed, and I'd rather you didn't go in. She gets so excited when she sees you."

"Too bad it doesn't run in the family," he answered impishly.

Granger obviously had no idea of the fireflies that were lighting up Melissa's midsection. She turned to Vivian. "I won't be late."

"That's all right. Stay out as long as you like," Vivian replied.

"I'll take your advice," Granger told her with a smile. "It's been nice meeting you, Vivian. I hope I'll see you again."

"I do, too," she answered fervently.

When they were in the car driving away, Melissa said, "As you must have noticed, Vivian is a big fan of yours."

"How can you tell? She didn't ask for my autograph," Granger joked.

"She was too overwhelmed. I've never seen Vivian that tongue-tied."

"People just like to meet so-called celebrities," he said dismissively.

"It's funny," Melissa mused. "I've gotten so used to you that I don't think of you as a celebrity."

Granger reached over and took her hand. "That's the nicest thing you've ever said to me."

"It's true. I wish you *were* just a normal man," she said wistfully.

"I am, honey." His hand tightened. "I'm a *very* normal man."

Melissa changed the subject hurriedly. "Where are we going for dinner?"

"I made reservations at the Chanticleer. Is that all right?"

"Fabulous. Vivian will be so impressed. She'll want to know every single detail, including what we had to eat."

Granger smiled. "Do you intend to tell her everything we do tonight?"

"Is there any reason why I shouldn't?" Melissa asked lightly.

"A leading question if I ever heard one," he murmured. "Can I get back to you on that later?"

Before she could think of a clever response, Granger nosed into the curb in front of a restaurant with a striped awning extending to the street. A young man in a red jacket opened Melissa's door, and another parking attendant raced around to Granger's side of the car.

"Good evening, Mr. McMasters," he said. "Good to see you back."

The foyer of the restaurant was crowded with stylishly dressed patrons waiting for tables. In spite of their sophistication, a buzz went through the throng and they all stared at Granger avidly.

The maître d' approached to lead them inside. "So nice to see you, Mr. McMasters. Your table is ready."

As they followed the man, Granger was hailed from several different tables. Melissa recognized a few celebrities in the groups, plus many people who weren't familiar but looked important.

"I hope this table is satisfactory, Mr. McMasters." The maître d' seated Melissa and placed a large white linen napkin on her lap with a flourish.

"It's fine, André," Granger replied.

After beckoning imperiously, the man left them, but a bevy of other men answered his summons. A busboy filled their water glasses, a wine steward with a chain around his neck arrived with the wine list, and their waiter stood by with large tasseled menus. All except the busboy addressed Granger by name.

"I believe we'll have a drink before we decide," Granger told the other two men.

"Very good, Mr. McMasters," the waiter said. "May I just tell you that we have orange roughy flown in this morning from Australia. I'll put two orders aside in case you should want it."

When everyone had departed, Melissa remarked, "If the food is as good as the service, it's no wonder they're so crowded."

Granger shrugged. "The food does happen to be good, but that's not what draws people. They come here to see and be seen."

"That doesn't sound like you."

"No, I come because even though I'm recognized, nobody bothers me."

While it was true that no one was gauche enough to ask for his autograph, a steady stream of people stopped at their table. Some only came to say hello and engage in a little chitchat. They were the ones who inspected Melissa with barely concealed curiosity. She could see the speculation in their eyes, when Granger introduced her and they didn't recognize her name.

The producers, directors and writers who stopped by were a different matter. They couldn't have cared less about her, although they were polite. Granger was their real target. They all had a project they were trying to interest him in.

A smooth-looking man in an expensive dark suit was especially persistent. He pulled up a chair and sat down at their table. Alan Brandenburg was a well-known producer. Even Melissa recognized his name.

"This is a stroke of luck," he said to Granger. "I was going to phone you tomorrow."

"Why don't you do that?" Granger asked, a trifle pointedly.

"We can talk now as long as I have you here."

"Melissa and I are having dinner."

The man was undeterred. "Go right ahead. I'll do the talking."

"Not now, Alan," Granger said. "I'm sure Melissa wouldn't be interested in shop talk. She isn't in the industry."

"I'll only keep him a few minutes," the producer promised her, turning back to Granger immediately. "Max said he sent you the Newmark script, *Avenging Justice.* What did you think of it?"

"You don't really want to know," Granger answered wryly.

"How can you say that? It's a natural for you—crusading attorney, terrific love interest. Marilyn Stanhope is ready to commit, and I think I can get Roy Wainwright to direct."

"The script is a hack job," Granger said succinctly.

"So we'll do a rewrite. I'll get Mark Jennings. He's hot right now, and he's available. His latest flick is in answer print."

"Tolstoy couldn't doctor that script."

"Trust me," Alan soothed. "You haven't even heard the deal I'm prepared to offer. How does five gross points from break sound?"

Granger raised an eyebrow. "Not good when your number crunchers get finished."

"This is a legitimate deal point offer, I swear to you. No rolling break."

Melissa listened in bewilderment to the foreign terms. Millions of dollars were being discussed, and she couldn't understand one word they were saying.

Granger tried to end the conversation. "I'm not interested, Alan, and this is very boring for Melissa."

"Okay, I'll let you finish your dinner if you'll promise to give it some more thought," Alan said.

They were joined by another man with the same stylish haircut and impeccably tailored dark suit. Were movie executives cloned somewhere, Melissa wondered? This one's name was Perry Golden, and he was head of a large studio. He also pulled up a chair without being invited.

Throughout dinner, various people either stood or sat at their table. Some were directors, one was a writer, and several were simply people who wanted others in the restaurant to think they were friendlier with Granger than was actually the case.

During one of the rare periods when they were alone, Melissa asked, "Is it always like this when you go out to dinner?"

"I'm sorry," Granger apologized. "I wanted this to be such a nice evening, but you're not having a very good time."

"I wasn't complaining. I merely wondered if this was the norm."

"It's a little crazier than usual tonight," he admitted. "Probably because I'm between pictures. A lot of people have projects to push."

"It must be gratifying to be in such demand."

"For now," he answered cynically. "Everybody wants you when you're on top. If your numbers start to slip, you can't get the office boy to return your phone calls."

"That must be a scary prospect," Melissa said slowly.

"Not to me. I've always known the bubble could burst someday."

"What would you do then?"

"Any number of things. I have a cattle ranch in Colorado. A foreman runs it for me now, but I've always thought I'd like to be a working owner."

Melissa could see Granger in the role. His dark hair would blow becomingly across his tanned forehead as he controlled a spirited horse, eyes narrowed in concentration. Granger would handle the job of cowboy as masterfully as he did everything else.

Their interlude of privacy didn't last long. Once again they had company. Granger did his best to speed them on their way, with little result. He also kept trying to include Melissa in the conversation, but that wasn't a success, either.

While the visitors talked about people she didn't know, Melissa ate her dinner. At least the food was delicious and innovative. Her saltimbocca was layered with pancetta instead of prosciutto, in addition to a creamy cheese of some variety.

Dessert was pure ambrosia. A mound of chocolate bavarian cream was ringed by thin slices of fresh pineapple and dollops of whipped cream topped with red raspberries. Melissa was scraping her plate clean while Granger's plate remained barely touched. That had been the pattern throughout all the courses.

"No wonder you stay so trim," she commented unexpectedly. "You never get a chance to eat."

It was her first remark in some time. The people standing around Granger looked startled, as though that had never occurred to them. After a few moments they left.

"I'm sorry if I was rude," Melissa told Granger calmly. "But *their* manners leave a lot to be desired. You'd be better off with autograph seekers. At least they don't hang around forever."

"You weren't rude," he assured her. "You were remarkably patient. What can I do to make it up to you?"

"Eat your dessert. It's delicious."

"Did you enjoy your dinner, at least?"

"It was wonderful. I had a lovely time, honestly." She really had, in an offbeat sort of way. It was interesting to meet the many famous and powerful people she'd read about—if only they hadn't stayed so long.

"The evening isn't over yet. How would you like to go dancing at the Rock Exchange?" He named a disco currently popular with people who made the news.

"I don't think so, Granger. I told Vivian I wouldn't be late."

"It's only ten-thirty."

"I know, but by the time we get out of here and you drive me home, it will be a lot later."

"Don't give up on me, Melissa." He reached over and took her hand. "I promise the rest of the evening will be different. Let me take you someplace where we can talk. We've barely had a minute alone together."

"It would be the same anywhere else." She sighed. "The only place we've ever had a quiet conversation is at your house or mine."

"That's an idea. Let's go to my place for an after-dinner drink."

"I wasn't suggesting that."

"I know, but it's the perfect answer." Granger signaled for the check.

Melissa let herself be persuaded, even though she had very real doubts about the wisdom of what she was doing. She'd wanted all evening to be alone with Granger, but not *completely* alone. Things had gotten out of hand between them before, in broad daylight with Mrs. Flannery within earshot. Melissa could imagine how romantic the atmosphere would be tonight, lit by moonlight and scented with roses.

Granger seemed unaware of her reservations. He kept up a steady flow of conversation on the drive to his home.

Melissa felt strange as she followed him inside. "I've never been in your house before," she commented.

"Really? Let me turn on some lights and I'll show you around."

Granger led her through one beautifully furnished room after another. The living room was huge and elegant, while the den that backed it was more informal. Large couches and chairs looked comfortable, and books lined one wall. Wide sliding glass doors opened to the terrace and pool area.

"What a lovely room," Melissa said. "I'll bet you spend most of your time here."

"You're right."

He showed her the intricate entertainment center. Behind handsome oak panels was an elaborate stereo system, television screen and a lot of other electronic equipment. Matching paneled doors on another wall opened to reveal a built-in wet bar, abundantly stocked.

"What can I fix you to drink?" he asked.

"Surprise me."

A little smile tilted his firm mouth. "Is that what you really want?"

"I'll have whatever you're having." She continued hurriedly, "Your home is beautiful."

"I'm glad you like it." Granger concealed his amusement as he handed her a crystal snifter containing an amber liquid. "Is brandy all right?"

"Fine, thank you."

He raised his glass. "Here's to peace and quiet. It's wonderful."

"This is certainly a change from the restaurant. I knew you were a big name, but I never realized all that entailed."

"The loss of privacy?" Granger shrugged. "You take the bitter with the better."

She glanced around the luxurious room. "There are certainly compensations."

"And drawbacks. I waited so long to get a date with you. I wanted tonight to be special." His voice deepened a note.

"It was for me. I couldn't even have gotten into that restaurant tonight. Or at least, I wouldn't have received such royal treatment. It was a revelation to see how the other half lives." Melissa knew she was babbling, but the quiet house and the glow in Granger's eyes was making her nerves quiver.

"Is that all that made tonight special?" he asked.

"Didn't you have enough adulation for one evening?" she countered lightly.

"That's not what I'm looking for from you." He stroked her cheek with a feathery touch.

"I *know* what you want from me," she said dryly.

"Do you, Melissa? I don't think so. You're unlike any woman I've ever known. Of course I want to make love to you. I've admitted that openly. But I want more than that. You're like a breath of fresh air in my life. I enjoy just being with you and hearing you laugh."

Melissa's heart soared. Was it possible that Granger cared about more than simply getting her into bed? It was hard to believe, but his voice throbbed with sincerity. As she gazed up at him tremulously, the phone rang.

A look of annoyance crossed his handsome face. "Ignore it. The answering machine will pick up."

The strident sound was hard to ignore. They both paused, waiting for it to stop. After several rings the machine clicked on and a woman's voice was audible after the beep.

"It's Chloe, Mac. I have to talk to you. It's really urgent. Please call me, no matter when you get home."

Halfway through her message, Granger started toward the phone. "Excuse me for a moment. I'd better take this call," he told Melissa. His expression was concerned as he picked up the receiver. "I'm here, Chloe. What's the matter?"

Melissa didn't wait to hear any more. She went outside, feeling like a complete idiot. How could she have believed Granger when he said she was special to him? Until one of his other special little friends whistled for him. Granger was a great actor. This wasn't the first time she'd seen him in action. When he pulled out all the stops, he could make a woman feel she was the center of his universe.

But no more, Melissa vowed. She wasn't going to fall for his phony line again, no matter how convincing he sounded.

Chapter Five

Granger joined Melissa on the terrace a short time later. "I'm sorry, but a very dear friend of mine had a problem."

"That's too bad," Melissa answered evenly. "Did you solve it for her?"

"I tried. Shall we go inside? It's getting chilly out here. I don't want you to catch cold."

She returned to the den with him reluctantly. If she'd followed her inclination and asked him to take her home, Granger would think she cared about his phone call.

When they were seated on the couch he smiled at her. "I unplugged the phone so there won't be any more interruptions."

"You didn't need to do that. We weren't discussing anything important."

"Whatever you say is of interest to me," he answered smoothly.

"You're the one who's led a full life." Melissa was determined not to let him get personal. "How did you become a movie star?"

"Accidentally. I was working at a dude ranch during spring break at college. A film company came there to shoot a B movie, and they hired me to do some riding."

"So you didn't have to go knocking on doors. You were discovered."

Granger chuckled. "It wasn't quite that easy. Years of hard work intervened before I learned my craft and started to get decent parts. Years that my parents considered wasted, I might add. They feel the same way you do about the entertainment industry."

"What did they want you to be?"

"Something more respectable," he said with amusement. "My father is a physician, and my mother is the principal of a girls' school. What I do is frivolous to them."

"Surely they're proud of you now, though."

"Let's say they're resigned. I won't achieve complete approval until I settle down and present them with a couple of grandchildren."

"Are you an only child?"

"No, I have two married brothers who have three children between them. The fact that they're younger than I doesn't help my case."

"You're very fortunate to have a family," Melissa said wistfully. "I'm an only child, and my parents died when I was still in high school."

"That's rough," Granger said sympathetically. "Who looked after you?"

"An aunt and uncle took me in, but they had four children of their own. They did their best, but I never really felt like I belonged."

"I'm sorry," he said in a muted voice.

"It's all part of the past. I've often wondered, though, if that's why I got married so young," she mused.

"You must have had Betsy right away."

"Stan and I were married when I graduated from high school, and she was born nine and a half months later." Melissa smiled humorlessly. "Birth control was one of the many things I learned the hard way."

"Surely your husband—" Granger cut his explosive comment short.

"He considered that my department."

No one had told her that birth-control pills weren't effective immediately. If Stan knew it, he was willing to take the chance rather than inconvenience himself. Although he was less than happy with the result.

"The more I find out about him, the less I like the guy," Granger said disgustedly. "What did you see in him in the first place?"

"He said he loved me." Melissa's mouth twisted wryly. "I was a pushover for affection in those days."

"You poor kid." Granger's voice vibrated with emotion.

"You don't have to feel sorry for me. I had unrealistic expectations of marriage. From all the evidence around, men aren't naturally monogamous."

"You're judging all men by one jerk who let you down?"

"Once was enough."

"You were young and innocent then," he said impatiently. "You weren't really in love with him."

"It still hurt when he walked out on me."

"Of course it did! But you have to forget about him."

"I have. I don't know why I'm talking about Stan tonight. I honestly never think of him."

"That would be fine if he hadn't left a scar." Granger smoothed the silky hair away from her face. "Don't be afraid to let someone else into your life. You're a warm, vibrant woman. You can't go on stifling all your normal emotions."

"I don't," she protested.

"Show me," he said softly.

Granger drew her into his arms and kissed her tenderly. When Melissa stiffened in alarm, he murmured soothing words and dropped butterfly kisses over her cheeks, her closed eyelids, the corner of her trembling mouth.

"You're so exquisite," he said huskily. "Let me show you how it should be."

Melissa's mind sounded a warning, but her body refused to listen. Granger's seductive mouth was too alluring. She wanted to wrap her arms around his neck and surrender to the hot tide of longing that was sweeping through her. Tentatively, she touched his cheek with her fingertips.

"Yes, angel," he murmured. "You see how easy it is?"

His lips parted hers for a kiss that made her tremble. She clung to him, wanting more, *needing* more. When he drew her even closer and their bodies conformed, she uttered a tiny cry of pleasure.

"I knew there was passion under all that restraint," he said with satisfaction.

His words penetrated her fevered brain. "No, I—you're wrong."

How could she have allowed this to happen? Melissa drew back. When he didn't release her, she braced her palms against his hard chest to keep a small distance between their bodies.

"Why are you so afraid of human contact?" he asked gently.

"What you were leading up to is more familiar than I want to get," she answered tautly.

"I could prove you're wrong." One arm continued to circle her waist while he slowly traced the wide neckline of her dress.

Melissa became rigid. "I can't believe you won't take no for an answer."

He released her immediately. "Did your husband force himself on you, in addition to all his other sins?"

"Stan has nothing to do with this."

"I think he does. He's turned you off so completely that any honest display of affection repels you."

"That's not true." She was glad Granger didn't know how mistaken he was.

"Why not admit it?" He gazed at her downcast lashes. "For a moment there, you wanted me as much as I wanted you. But whenever a man touches you too intimately, you flash back to Stan's aggression."

Perhaps it would have been better to let Granger think she was frigid, but Melissa was unwilling to do that. Her feelings toward him were confusing in the extreme.

She jumped up from the couch, her cheeks flushed. "The reason I won't let you make love to me isn't that complicated. You're very attractive. I don't have to tell you that. I simply don't want to get involved."

"You've made *that* perfectly clear," he answered dryly.

"Then your feelings shouldn't be hurt."

"My ego isn't suffering. What puzzles me is why you're suppressing your perfectly normal desires. Since I know your views on involvement, there wouldn't be any strings attached."

"I didn't expect there would be—not on your part, anyway."

Granger lounged back on the couch, watching her like a deceptively tame tiger. "As long as you're not looking for a permanent arrangement, why not me? You've admitted you don't find me repulsive, and I'm irresistibly attracted to *you*." His smile held great charm.

"For how long? You're merely intrigued because I've held out so long. Next week or next month you'll be saying the same thing to some other woman."

Granger got up with feline grace. He sauntered over and combed his fingers through her long hair. "That should relieve your mind. You wouldn't have to worry about my hanging around indefinitely."

She jerked her head away. "I don't indulge in casual affairs."

"Our romance might be short and sweet, but I promise it wouldn't be casual." His voice was very soft.

"I think you'd better take me home," Melissa said carefully.

"You don't have to go. I'm not going to sulk." He laughed unexpectedly.

Had Granger only been teasing her all along? Or didn't he care that much one way or the other? Neither alternative pleased her.

"Vivian will be expecting me," she said. "I really have to go."

"All right, if you insist."

Granger got her coat from the guest closet and helped her on with it. Before she could move away, he wrapped his arms around her from behind. When she tilted her head to protest, he kissed the tip of her nose.

"Our first date wasn't very successful, was it, honey? And don't say this is the first *and* last one, because I have no intention of losing you."

She was extremely conscious of the enveloping embrace that nestled her body against his, spoon fashion. "I'm not going to change my mind." Melissa hoped she sounded firm.

"Then I'll just have to be a good loser. We can't let sex break up a beautiful friendship." He smiled. "Come on, I'll take you home."

The fact that Granger gave up so cheerfully proved how little he cared. Melissa told herself she was grateful. Their friendship had a better chance of lasting than a love affair did.

Vivian was wide awake and waiting to hear every detail of the big date with Granger. Melissa concentrated on the restaurant and the famous people she'd met, hoping that would be enough. She didn't want to tell Vivian that she'd gone back to Granger's house, knowing her friend would jump to conclusions.

"I told you a date with him would be exciting," Vivian said.

"It was more like an evening with *Who's Who in Hollywood.* I barely got to say two words to Granger during dinner."

"But you got to meet all those big names. How about afterward? Did he kiss you good-night?"

"Briefly." That was factual. Granger's parting kiss was little more than a friendly peck. "Did Betsy wake up for anything?"

"She slept like a baby."

"That's good. I really want to thank you for baby-sitting, Viv. I'm sorry I stayed out later than I expected. You must want to get home."

Vivian didn't take the hint. "There's no hurry. Where did you go afterward?"

"It, uh, was a long dinner."

"You couldn't have been at the restaurant until now. It doesn't stay open this late."

"We went back to Granger's house for a nightcap," Melissa said reluctantly, realizing that Vivian would keep asking questions until she found out.

"Aha! Now we're getting to the good part."

"Don't be silly. We had one drink, talked a little and he brought me home."

"He didn't make even a tiny pass?"

"No." Melissa wasn't a good liar. Her pink cheeks gave her away.

"Don't hand me that. I can tell just by looking at you that you're holding something back. Granger didn't get his reputation as a great lover for nothing."

"I wouldn't know."

"You mean you didn't make love. But something must have happened, or you wouldn't look so guilty."

Melissa couldn't allow Vivian's imagination to run wild. "All right, he kissed me. It was no big deal. I told him I wasn't interested in having an affair, and that was that."

"You actually turned down Granger McMasters?"

"Of course I did. Would *you* go to bed with someone just because he's a celebrity?"

"I don't know if I could resist him. Being famous has nothing to do with it—or not very much, anyway. He's simply the most spectacular male I've ever seen."

"You sound like a bobby-soxer."

"I can't help it. When I met him in person tonight, I turned to jelly. That man has charm! He makes a woman feel as if she's special."

"Whatever woman he happens to be with at the time," Melissa said grimly.

"I suppose so, but wouldn't it be nice to have his full attention for one night?" Vivian asked wistfully.

"Not when you knew you were just a warm body in his bed, another notch on the old bedpost."

"He didn't strike me as a typical Hollywood sleaze ball," Vivian objected.

"He isn't," Melissa admitted. "Granger has been really nice to Betsy and me, and that's all the more reason for steering clear of him."

"I suppose you're right. It could cause complications." Vivian sighed. "But haven't you ever wondered, in your secret fantasies, what it would be like?"

"No, I haven't." Melissa took off her shoes and dangled them from one hand. "It's late. We both have to work tomorrow."

"You're right." Vivian gathered her things together. "Well, let me know if anything develops."

"It won't."

Vivian's words rang in Melissa's ears as she got undressed. Haven't you ever wondered what it would be like? Of course she had, now more than ever. Each encounter with Granger brought new evidence of his virility. Her softer body had yielded to his hard male angles, and she'd experienced the devastation his sensuous mouth could bring. Melissa knew instinctively that Granger's full possession would be like nothing she'd ever known. His taut, thrusting body would bring the kind of rapture she'd only dreamed of.

When her eyes focused on her dazzled face in the bathroom mirror, she caught her breath and hurriedly turned off the light.

Melissa felt diffident when she went to Granger's house on Monday morning. That was the trouble with dating one's boss. It made their working relationship difficult.

Granger didn't share her ambivalence. His behavior was completely natural, as always. Nothing ever ruffled his poise. Or at least, *she* didn't, Melissa thought forlornly.

"Those impatiens you planted are still puny," he complained, inspecting the row of little plants.

"They've only been in for a few weeks. Give them a chance."

"I have a tendency to rush things—as you've probably noticed." He smiled.

Melissa turned away. "You can't hurry nature."

"If I'm patient, will I see results?" he asked softly.

"As long as your expectations aren't too high." She knelt on the grass and started to pull weeds.

"I've scaled them down." Granger didn't pretend they were talking about flowers. "Have dinner with me tonight and you can see for yourself."

"I can't ask Vivian to baby-sit again so soon."

"You still refuse to consider an agency?"

"I'd have to check them out first," Melissa answered vaguely.

"Okay, then I have an alternate suggestion. Bring Betsy over here when she gets home from school. I promised she could go swimming, and afterward I'll barbecue hamburgers."

Melissa sat back on her heels and looked up at him. "Why would you want to louse up an evening like that?

I'd have to take Betsy home by eight o'clock at the latest, and you'd be left at loose ends.''

"I'll come home with you, and we'll make out on your couch," he teased.

Melissa smiled reluctantly. "Betsy would be a big hit in school during show and tell."

"The *National Observer* would pay her for information like that, but I see your point. All right, we'll just have dinner, no hanky-panky."

"Are you sure you want to do this?" Melissa asked doubtfully.

"Positive. The only time I get to barbecue is on Mrs. Flannery's night off."

"She doesn't like you messing up her kitchen?"

"She's never complained, but she does all the preliminary work and then stands there and hands me everything I need, like a nurse assisting a doctor. It takes all the fun out of it."

"Don't knock it. I wouldn't mind being waited on hand and foot," Melissa commented.

"You will be tonight," he promised. "I'll go in and phone the market. What else do kids like besides hamburgers?"

Betsy was in awe of Granger's imposing house and spacious grounds. She glanced around wide-eyed. "Do you live here all alone?"

"Not completely. I have a housekeeper named Mrs. Flannery who lives with me."

"Does she have her own bedroom?"

"Yes." Granger smiled.

"Mom and I share a bedroom."

"You're very fortunate." He shot an amused glance at Melissa.

"If you want to go swimming you'd better go in now before it starts to cool off," Melissa told her daughter hastily.

"Are you coming in, too?" Betsy included Granger in the query.

"You bet." He turned to Melissa. "You know where the bathing suits are."

"I brought my own this time," she answered.

"Maybe it's just as well. I have to be on my good behavior today," he murmured.

"I'm counting on it," she told him.

Betsy had her suit on under her jeans and was already stripping off her clothes by the side of the pool. Melissa gathered them up and went into the cabana to change.

When she came out, Granger was in the water with Betsy. She had her arms around his neck and was clinging like a limpet to his back as he swam with her to the deep end.

"Guess what, Mom?" Betsy called excitedly when she saw her mother. "Mac is going to teach me to jump off the diving board."

Melissa sat on the edge and watched as they romped in the pool. After Granger brought Betsy back to the shallow end, they played catch with a gaily colored, inflated ball. He seemed to be enjoying himself as much as the little girl, whose face was alight with pleasure.

This was the kind of father Betsy deserved, Melissa thought poignantly. Someone who cared about her and took time to play with her. That was one of the many things she couldn't give her daughter.

Granger swam over and clasped Melissa's ankles where they dangled under the water. "What's wrong? You're not having a good time."

She mustered a smile. "What gave you that idea?"

"You look sad."

"You're imagining things. Come on, let's make it three-way catch."

He put his hands on her waist to prevent her from jumping into the pool "Tell me about it, honey. I'm very good at solving problems."

Granger didn't know he's created this one. Melissa hadn't dreamed there were men like him in the world. She tried to erase the troubled thoughts from her face.

"If I ever have a problem I'll keep you in mind," she said lightly.

"Promise?" His arms circled her waist.

She put her hands on his shoulders to hold him off—unnecessarily because he was merely pulling her into the pool. Granger's intentions might have been innocent, but her breasts were scant inches from his mouth as her body slid the length of his. The erotic feeling was disturbing enough, but when the cool water hit her sun-warmed skin, she flinched instinctively, arching into him.

Granger's embrace tightened, and suddenly Melissa wasn't so sure about his intentions. "Is this what you consider good behavior?" she demanded.

"No, but it's the best I can do under the circumstances." He grinned.

She disentangled herself without comment and swam over to Betsy.

The sun was going down by the time Melissa persuaded the little girl to get out of the pool.

"You can come back again," Granger assured her.

"When?" Betsy asked promptly.

"When Mac invites you," Melissa answered before he could.

After a look at her mother's face, Betsy followed her docilely to the cabana. She was soon distracted by the dressing room with its wardrobe of bathing suits and abundant supply of beauty products.

"How come Mac has all this perfume and stuff? Men don't use that."

"Those things are for guests."

"He must know a lot of ladies," Betsy decided.

"I think that's a safe assumption," Melissa replied dryly.

"Why doesn't Mac have a wife, Mom?"

"I don't know."

"I'm going to ask him."

"No, you're not," Melissa said swiftly. "It isn't polite to ask personal questions."

"Then how do you ever find out things you want to know?" Betsy complained.

"You wait until you're told." Melissa switched on the hair dryer.

Granger was poking at the coals in an elaborate barbecue on the terrace in front of the pool house. He glanced up and smiled. "Don't you both look nice."

"We washed our hair, and Mom used some of that perfume you have in there for all the ladies you know," Betsy volunteered. When Melissa looked at her sharply, she said in an injured tone, "I didn't ask him anything personal. *You* said he knew lots of ladies."

Granger chuckled. "What was it you weren't supposed to ask me?"

"Don't encourage her." Melissa frowned. "What can we do to help?"

"Nothing right now. Everything is ready to go on the grill, but we have time for a drink while the coals burn down."

"Can I bring the food from the house?" Melissa asked.

"I did that earlier. It's all in the refrigerator," he gestured toward the cabana.

The sliding glass doors were open, revealing a large, casually furnished room. Behind a bar that divided off one end of the room was a compact kitchen.

Betsy was intrigued. "You have a big house and a little house. Why is that?"

"This one is for guests," Granger explained. "Or just for people who want to get in out of the sun for a while."

"Can I look inside?" she asked.

"Go right ahead."

"You've made a real conquest," Melissa told him. "Betsy thinks you're the greatest."

"I'd like to think the opinion is unanimous," he said with a smile.

"You have plenty of women on your team. It's more of an accomplishment to win the unqualified approval of a seven-year-old."

"She's a nifty kid. I wouldn't mind having a houseful just like her."

"Betsy is one of a kind," Melissa said fondly.

"You did such a good job with her, you should have more children."

Melissa shook her head. "I'm not that liberated a woman."

"I wasn't suggesting you go it alone. This time you should have a husband who'd also be a father."

Melissa flashed back to Granger and Betsy romping in the pool. She closed her mind to the futile thought. "You know my views on the subject," she answered carelessly.

Betsy came racing out of the house. "You know what? Mac's got video games in there. Can I play with them?"

"That's what they're for," he replied indulgently.

"Maybe it was a mistake to bring her here," Melissa remarked ruefully when Betsy had run off again. "Your toys are fancier than hers."

"My mother taught me to share." He smiled. "You're welcome anytime."

"I want to thank you for devoting so much time to her, Granger. Betsy never had this kind of attention."

"You both deserve better than you got," he said huskily. "I'm happy if I can make things a little better."

"You have, but it's made me feel guilty. I'm depriving her of something she's entitled to."

"Guilt is scarcely an adequate reason for marrying again."

"That's what I've always felt."

Granger watched her with an unreadable expression for a moment. Then he rose to his feet. "I promised you a drink, didn't I? What would you like?"

When the coals had burned down to a ruddy glow, Granger put hamburger patties on the grill. While they sizzled, sending forth an appetizing aroma, Melissa set the round table on the patio and brought the rest of the food from the refrigerator.

Betsy left the video games reluctantly. "Can I play some more after dinner?" she asked.

"While we're cleaning up," Melissa answered. "After that we have to go home."

"It's still early," Betsy objected.

"It won't be by the time you get to bed. Tomorrow is a school day."

"How is your hamburger?" Granger asked, to distract her.

"Great! This tastes even better than Mom's."

"That's high praise." He smiled. "Your mother is a good cook."

"This tastes different, though."

"Because it's grilled instead of broiled," he explained.

"Could we get a barbecue?" Betsy asked Melissa.

"I don't know where we'd put it," she answered. "You have to barbecue outside, and we don't have a yard."

"You could keep a small-sized grill outside your kitchen door," Granger suggested.

"I'm not sure the landlord would approve," Melissa said doubtfully.

"He's real mean," Betsy said.

Melissa looked at her in surprise. "Mr. Davidson has never given us any trouble. Why would you say a thing like that?"

"He won't let us have a dog."

"A lot of landlords don't allow dogs."

"How about a parakeet or a hamster instead?" Granger asked.

"It says no pets in the lease," Melissa answered regretfully when Betsy looked suddenly hopeful.

Granger concealed his pity as he gazed at the small girl's crestfallen face. "I have an idea. What if I bought a dog and we shared him?"

Betsy was intrigued, yet uncertain about the feasibility. "How could we do that?"

"I'll keep him here, and you can come over and play with him."

"I'd like to, but he wouldn't really be mine."

"Sure he would. We'll sign a contract, sort of like the lease your mother signed. It will say we're equal partners. That means you have to take your share of the responsibility, though," Granger warned.

"Like what?"

"You'll have to brush him and throw a ball for him so he gets his exercise. When you own an animal, you have to take care of it."

"Oh, I will! I promise!" Betsy's face lit up like a Christmas tree.

Melissa had been listening with growing concern. "Mac is being very generous, but if he does buy a dog, you won't actually own any part of it," she told her.

"He says I will," Betsy replied stubbornly.

"He's only trying to be kind, but his efforts are misguided. You mustn't mislead her, Granger."

After a glance at Melissa's troubled face and the child's rebellious one, he said to Betsy, "Why don't you go back to your video game and let me straighten this out with your mother." When they were alone he asked Melissa, "What's the problem?"

"I know you meant well, but I've never promised Betsy things she couldn't have."

"So?" He gave her a puzzled frown.

"So, leading her to believe she's getting a dog is a hoax."

"I fully intend to buy one. I've been thinking about it since our discussion."

"I'm not questioning that. All I'm saying is, you shouldn't have deceived her into thinking she'll have a claim on him."

"Aren't you making a big deal out of nothing? Betsy wants a dog, and this is the only way she can have one right now."

"Don't you understand? She thinks she'll be able to visit him regularly."

"I don't have a problem with that." Granger smiled.

"Maybe not now, but what happens when things change?"

"What things?"

"I realize you're...sort of interested in me at the present time," Melissa began hesitantly.

"What gave me away?" He grinned. "When I said I wanted to make love to you?"

"This is serious, Granger. You've been wonderful to Betsy and me, and I don't believe it was out of any ulterior motive. I like to think you've enjoyed being with us. Maybe just because of the novelty of the situation, it doesn't matter."

"Don't sell yourself short," he advised.

"Well, anyway, what I'm saying is, I don't delude myself that your interest in me will continue."

"I never thought that would bother you," he remarked casually.

"It doesn't, unless it affects Betsy. I'm concerned about what will happen when you get involved with someone else."

"Someone *else?* I'd say *our* relationship is about as chaste as it could get," he said dryly.

"That's why I know you'll be moving on soon. And when you do, I don't want Betsy to get hurt."

"You lost me. What does Betsy have to do with my love life?"

"Having a seven-year-old underfoot isn't exactly conducive to romance—especially when I'd have to bring her over here. You won't want the two of us hanging around, and I certainly don't want to be here while you're entertaining another woman."

"Let me get this straight. Are you worried about Betsy's feelings or your own?" His eyes were narrowed as he waited for her reaction.

"I couldn't care less about whom you see or what you do with her," Melissa replied angrily.

Granger looked perversely pleased by her answer. "In that case we don't have any problem," he said smoothly.

"You're handing me a king-size one. How will I explain to Betsy that she isn't welcome here anymore?"

"That will never happen. If your worst scenario comes true, I promise to restrain my lust in front of your daughter." He looked amused.

"I can tell you're not taking this seriously." Melissa's generous mouth was compressed in a straight line.

"You worry enough for both of us," he answered mildly.

"I know how much pain rejection can cause."

Granger's amusement vanished and he reached for her hand. "I told you I'd never hurt you, and I meant it. That goes for Betsy, too. Won't you try to trust me just a little bit?"

"You haven't left me any choice," she said helplessly.

He smiled wryly. "That's not exactly a rousing vote of confidence, but it's a step in the right direction."

"Will you at least promise to check with me in the future before you mention any of these brainstorms of yours in front of Betsy? You make it almost impossible for me to say no to her."

"Why can't I have the same effect on you?" he teased.

"Your requests are unreasonable."

"I'm willing to negotiate."

"Don't you think I've been flexible enough for one day?" Melissa rose and started gathering up the plates.

"You're making definite signs of progress. The next thing we have to do is work on your inhibitions."

"That's going to take more time than we have tonight." She gestured toward the bowl of potato salad. "Shall I take the leftovers up to the house?"

"No, they can go in the refrigerator here. At least you realize there's a lot of work to be done—on your inhibitions, I mean." He followed her into the cabana.

Betsy looked up from her game. "Is it okay? Did you talk to her, Mac?"

"Everything is settled," he assured her with a mischievous glance at Melissa. "You and I are getting a dog, and your mother is getting a front-row seat at my next amatory dalliance."

"What does that mean?" Betsy asked doubtfully.

"Pay no attention. Your friend Mac has a warped sense of humor," Melissa told her tartly. "You'd better start gathering your things together now."

Betsy was drooping by the time Melissa got her home and into bed. The excitement of the evening had worn off, leaving her tired but happy.

She smiled blissfully as Melissa tucked the covers around her. "Mac is a great guy, isn't he, Mom?"

"Yes, he is," Melissa agreed softly.

"I don't remember my dad very much. Was he like Mac?"

"No, he was different." Melissa bent to kiss her goodnight. "Go to sleep, honey."

Her thoughts were somber as she went into the living room. Betsy was becoming much too attached to Granger, and matters would only get worse when their lives were complicated by a dog. Worse for both herself and Betsy. Granger was only joking tonight about finding a new love, but it would happen inevitably. And she'd be an unwilling spectator.

Heaving a giant sigh, Melissa picked up a book.

Chapter Six

Melissa drove to Granger's house on Wednesday morning, trying to decide whether to spray the roses that day or wait until Friday. The weather report predicted possible overnight showers. As she got out of her car, preoccupied with the problem, a large furry object came hurtling toward her.

"Stay, Clancy!" Granger was racing after the dog, an overgrown, exuberant puppy. "Brace yourself, Melissa. He doesn't know his own strength."

The dog flung himself at her, waving his long plumy tail and barking excitedly. While Melissa laughingly tried to fend him off, he bestowed slurpy kisses on her with his long pink tongue.

Granger reached them and grabbed the dog's collar. "He's only four months old," he said apologetically.

"What's he going to be when he grows up? A pony?" Melissa squatted on her haunches to inspect the wriggling Irish setter pup. "He's gorgeous, Granger. Where did you get him?"

"From an actress I worked with once. She bought him because her boyfriend liked dogs, but then she changed boyfriends."

"Don't tell me." Melissa grinned. "The new boyfriend preferred cats?"

"Who knows? Anyway, he's a fantastic animal. Or at least he will be," Granger added as the puppy chewed on the cuff of Melissa's jeans. "I plan to send him to obedience school."

"The sooner the better." She chuckled.

"Do you think Betsy will like him? I intended to let her make the selection, but when I heard that Paulette was getting rid of Clancy, I couldn't resist."

"Betsy will adore him. I'd better not break the news until the weekend, though. She'll be wild to see him."

"Why don't you bring her over after school today?"

"Are you sure you want her back so soon?"

"I enjoyed having both of you on Monday. This place finally seemed like a home instead of a Hollywood set."

"You might regret the loss of that perfection," Melissa warned. "Wait until Clancy starts digging holes in the flower beds and Betsy knocks over something in your perfect pool house."

"Things can be replaced," he said dismissively. "Bring her over and we'll have an early dinner again."

"I thought you only barbecued on Mrs. Flannery's day off."

"Right. We'll let her cook for us tonight."

At that moment the housekeeper approached them across the lawn. "Telephone for you, Mr. McMasters."

"I'll be right there," he called.

Clancy started to follow Granger to the house, then veered off toward the newcomer, wagging his tail. Mrs. Flannery put out her hand to ward him off.

Melissa smiled at the woman. "He's a little terror, isn't he?"

"I don't know what Mr. McMasters wants with the nasty thing." The older woman's thin lips were compressed tightly.

Melissa's smile vanished. "He's very fond of dogs."

She might have known Mrs. Flannery didn't like pets. The only living thing she *did* seem to like was Granger. The milk of human kindness had dried up in her long ago.

"They're nothing but a nuisance! It wouldn't be so bad if he'd keep him in the garage, but that animal has the run of the place. There'll be dog hairs all over the house," the woman predicted darkly.

"Since it isn't your house, I wouldn't worry," Melissa said flippantly.

"That's the trouble with people like you," Mrs. Flannery answered contemptuously. "All you're interested in is your paycheck. I take care of this place like it was my own home."

Melissa's eyes glittered, an indication of her rising temper. "A home is meant to be lived in."

"By people, not livestock!"

Melissa wanted to tell her that sometimes the latter were preferable to the former, but she controlled herself. "I suggest you get used to Clancy. He's here to stay."

"We'll just see about that," the housekeeper muttered. "I have something to say around here."

Granger returned carrying a yellow tennis ball to throw for the dog. "That was Bill Waxman," he told Melissa. "He said to say hello. At least he approves of *you*."

"Did you get another lecture?" she laughed.

"The same old broken record. When are you going back to work?" As Mrs. Flannery started to return to the house, Granger stopped her. "We'll be having guests for dinner tonight. Miss Fairfield and her daughter. Betsy is only seven, so don't make anything elaborate."

"Yes, sir." The housekeeper's neutral voice masked her displeasure.

Melissa waited until she was out of earshot before saying hesitantly, "Maybe dinner wasn't such a good idea, Granger. Mrs. Flannery isn't overly fond of me."

"I told you not to take it personally."

"But she's already upset over Clancy. She doesn't like dogs, either."

"She'll love him when she gets to know him. You'll see."

Melissa wasn't as certain. The older woman felt threatened by any intrusion into her tight little world, even by a dog. Mrs. Flannery would have preferred to keep Granger isolated from everything and everybody. In spite of her annoyance, Melissa couldn't help feeling sorry for the woman.

Betsy was enchanted with Clancy, as Melissa had known she would be. It was a case of mutual love at first sight. Clancy abandoned everyone else to follow the little girl wherever she went.

Melissa and Granger sat on the terrace before dinner, watching them frolic on the lawn. Betsy was throwing a ball for the dog, and Clancy was chasing it.

"Stay away from the flower beds," Melissa called.

"Let them have fun," Granger told her indulgently. "What are a few flowers?"

"You were the one who complained because the impatiens were too small."

"I've gotten my priorities straight." His expression was gentle as he gazed into the distance. "Look at them. Isn't that a picture?"

"Idyllic." Melissa's tone was ironic.

Granger glanced at her sharply. "You sound as if you have reservations."

"Not at the moment. But this isn't typical of everyday life. You're looking at an idealized version. In real life kids get cranky, and dogs get sick on the rug."

"Minor mishaps. Why are you so negative?"

"Not negative, realistic. In your make-believe world, family life is a nineteen fifties sitcom. The truth would send you into shock."

"You don't believe I could handle any problems that might arise?"

"The danger is that you don't expect any."

"You must think I live in a vacuum. I deal with problems constantly."

"And when you come home, you leave them at the studio. Children don't keep office hours."

"You're a hard woman to convince."

"Why try?" she asked lightly.

"I sometimes wonder," he answered, a trifle grimly.

Mrs. Flannery came onto the terrace. "Dinner is ready whenever you are, Mr. McMasters."

"We'll be right with you," he said.

"Betsy," Melissa called. "Come wash your hands for dinner."

The little girl came skipping across the grass with the dog beside her. "Are we going to have hamburgers again?"

"I don't know. Let's wait and see." As the dog started to follow them into the house, Melissa said, "Leave Clancy outside."

"He has to have dinner, too," Betsy objected.

"I fed him this afternoon before you got here," Granger told her.

"Can't he just come in and keep us company?" Betsy wheedled.

"No, he can't," Melissa stated.

"I don't see what harm it would do," Granger said mildly.

"It's your dog, but I really think you should train him right from the beginning," Melissa said.

"This is a special occasion," Granger answered, with a smile for Betsy.

Even though she thought he was making a mistake, Melissa didn't argue the point. When they reached the dining room she had further misgivings. On her one previous visit to the house she'd taken only a cursory glance at the gracious room with its long marble-topped table. Flanking the table were high-backed chairs upholstered in a rich, plum-colored damask that echoed the shades in the jewel-toned oriental rug under them. Melissa shuddered to think of anything spilling on the chairs or carpet.

Betsy was also a little daunted. "Boy, this is sure a big room," she commented.

"Don't you have a breakfast room?" Melissa asked Granger tentatively.

"Yes, I'll show it to you after dinner if you like."

"Perhaps it would be better if we ate in there tonight."

"The table is all set," he pointed out.

Granger settled the matter by pulling out Melissa's chair. Since there was nothing else she could do, she took her seat, hoping for the best.

At first Betsy was subdued by her elegant surroundings. The crystal chandelier overhead cast a muted glow on linen placemats and delicate china. Granger soon put her at ease, however, with questions about school and her friend Cathy.

When the first course was served, tomato soup accompanied by little corn muffins, Clancy barked and pawed at Betsy's skirt. Melissa stopped her as she was breaking off a piece of muffin to give him.

"Don't feed Clancy at the table."

Betsy looked to Granger for support, but this time he was no help. "Your mother is right. He has enough bad habits already."

"Take the dog outside and come right back," Melissa told her.

"Do I have to?" Betsy pleaded.

"I think he'll settle down," Granger intervened. After he spoke sternly to the pup, Clancy stopped begging and curled up at Betsy's feet. "You see? All you have to do is show them who's boss," Granger said.

"It also helps that his tummy is full, and he's tuckered out from playing all afternoon," Melissa remarked dryly.

Granger laughed. "Okay, he still goes to obedience school."

Mrs. Flannery served the delicious meal like a well-trained robot. When Melissa complimented her on the food, the woman accepted the praise coolly. The only time her austere expression softened was in response to Granger.

"An excellent dinner, Mrs. Flannery, as always," he said.

"Thank you, Mr. McMasters," she answered softly.

"I liked the lamb chops with that mint jelly," Betsy said.

The housekeeper removed her plate without comment and left the room. She returned a short time later with crystal bowls filled with chocolate mousse.

"Oh, boy!" Betsy's eyes lit up. "Chocolate pudding, my favorite."

For the second time, Mrs. Flannery failed to respond to her. She served the dessert in silence, but as she set Betsy's dish in front of her, she stepped on Clancy's tail.

The dog gave a sharp yelp and jumped up, jogging Betsy's elbow as she was lifting her glass of milk. Melissa watched in horror as the milk cascaded out of the glass onto the marble table and over the edge, onto the rug.

They were all frozen for a moment, then Melissa jumped up and started mopping up the puddle on the table with her napkin. The scene was chaotic. Clancy was barking excitedly, and everyone was talking at once.

"I couldn't help it," Betsy said apprehensively.

"Never mind that now. Run in the kitchen and get some paper towels," Melissa told her.

"These things happen." Granger tried to calm everyone down."

"This beautiful rug." The housekeeper was on her hands and knees, blotting up the milk. "It's ruined!"

"It can be cleaned. Why is everybody making a federal case out of a minor accident?"

"I'm really sorry, Granger," Melissa said.

"Don't worry about it. Let's have our dessert and forget about the entire matter."

After things returned to normal, Betsy finished her chocolate pudding as fast as possible, then asked to be excused. When permission was granted, she took Clancy and went outside.

Granger smiled at Melissa after the child had gone. "I admire your restraint. You're dying to say I told you so."

"I don't enjoy being right, but I've had more experience with children than you have. They spill things."

"It wasn't her fault. It was Clancy's. I should have listened to you."

"They're both better off in washable surroundings—at least until they get a little older. I'm afraid Mrs. Flannery was very upset."

"The house is not a museum. It's meant to be lived in. I can assure you this wasn't the first time something spilled on the rug, and it won't be the last."

"Not if you allow Clancy the run of the place," Melissa said wryly.

"Let's take our coffee out to the terrace and see what mischief he's into now."

A soft breeze was blowing, and the grounds looked like a picture postcard. Melissa hated to leave, but when the garden lights came on, signaling the approach of nightfall, she called to Betsy.

"You don't have to go yet," Granger protested. "It's still early."

Betsy joined them and added her objections. "Can't we stay a little longer? I'm teaching Clancy a trick."

"You have school tomorrow," Melissa reminded her. "You need your sleep."

"I get plenty of sleep," Betsy grumbled. "I want to play with Clancy some more."

"You can see him on Friday," Granger consoled her. "That isn't a school night, so you'll be able to stay later."

"Is it okay, Mom?" Betsy asked eagerly.

"Perhaps we'll come for an hour or two, but not for dinner," Melissa told her firmly. "Mac has a life of his own. We can't keep imposing on him."

"I'm not complaining." He smiled.

"Don't encourage her, Granger. She can't pop in whenever she likes. We have to set some ground rules. I think once a week would be more than generous—preferably on the weekend, when that's convenient for you."

"I only get to see Clancy once a week?" Betsy asked in outrage.

"Let me discuss it with your mother," Granger said. "Why don't we stick to our Friday plans with a slight change?" he asked Melissa. "Bring Betsy over in the afternoon, and then you and I will go out to dinner later."

"I can't. Vivian is on night duty this week."

"We can still come over after school, though, can't we?" Betsy asked anxiously.

"I suppose so." Melissa was reluctant to disappoint her.

"Here's another idea," Granger said. "Betsy can spend the night here. Mrs. Flannery will look after her."

"That's not part of her job." Melissa declined promptly. "I couldn't ask her to do that."

"You don't have to. I'll ask her. She won't mind."

"That would be neat, Mom. Can I?" Betsy asked.

Melissa couldn't very well tell her that Mrs. Flannery seemed to have taken an instant dislike to her. She didn't want to criticize the woman to Granger, either. But leaving Betsy overnight was out of the question.

"I don't think it's a very good idea," she said weakly.

"Why not?" Granger asked.

"Well . . . she's never slept away from home before."

"Then it's time to cut the apron strings," he observed dryly.

"It isn't only that. I'm afraid Mrs. Flannery doesn't feel too kindly toward children after tonight's disaster." Melissa put it as delicately as possible.

"I'll be real careful," Betsy promised.

"She can have dinner in the breakfast room if that will make you feel better," Granger said.

Melissa couldn't hold out against both of them. They had an answer to all her objections. Finally she was forced to give in, over very real apprehensions.

As she dressed for dinner that Friday night, Melissa was torn between anticipation toward the evening ahead and guilt at leaving her daughter in a sticky situation. Although Betsy was far from unhappy. When Melissa left to go home and change, Betsy and Granger were in the pool having a great time.

Maybe her fears were groundless, Melissa told herself. Mrs. Flannery's disapproval could have been directed at the dog, and Betsy had merely received the fallout. The older woman wasn't used to children, but she'd warm up. Everyone responded to Betsy.

Melissa sprayed herself with perfume and inspected her appearance in the full-length mirror on the bathroom door. The plum-colored sweater Vivian had knitted for her matched her slim skirt, making a chic, yet casual outfit.

Granger had proposed an elegant restaurant, but remembering their last experience, Melissa suggested pizza and a movie instead. After he was sure she really meant it, he was delighted.

Granger arrived in a sweater and slacks. The cardigan was cashmere, and his open-neck shirt was silk, but the

"But we have to settle this. You promised you'd check with me before you proposed any plans in front of Betsy."

"I don't see the problem. She's enjoying herself, and you would be, too, if you'd stop looking for things to worry about."

Melissa gave him a troubled look. "Am I being overly protective? I don't want to smother her, but I feel such a sense of responsibility. I'm all she has."

Granger reached across the table and squeezed her hand. "You've done everything right. Betsy is a terrific kid."

"It's been easy so far," Melissa said slowly. "But I know it won't always be this simple."

"Just take it one step at a time," Granger said soothingly. "I'll help if you'll let me."

She looked at him gratefully. "You're so calm and reasonable. You should have children of your own."

"I hope to someday."

His vague reference to the future didn't indicate any huge rush. Which wasn't surprising. What sort of woman would Granger ultimately marry? Someone as glamorous as himself, no doubt.

Melissa looked at her watch abruptly. "We'd better get going if we want to get to the show on time."

As they drove to the theater she remarked, "This is like a busman's holiday for you. Are you sure you wouldn't rather do something else?"

"Very sure. I enjoy movies. Sitting in the audience is totally different from being in front of the camera."

"When do you think you'll go back to work?"

"I'm not in any hurry." He turned his head to smile at her. "Life has gotten more interesting at home lately."

"You should have bought a dog sooner," she commented lightly.

"I think my timing was just right," he said with satisfaction.

After the movie Granger suggested they go somewhere for a drink, but Melissa declined. "Let's not push our luck," she said. "Nobody's pestered you for an autograph so far."

"It's been a great night for me, but not too eventful for you, I'm afraid."

"You're wrong. This was quite an improvement over my usual evenings in front of the TV set."

"That has to be by choice." He gazed appreciatively at her delicate profile. "You could be out every night if you wanted to be. How did *I* get so lucky?"

She smiled ruefully. "You don't take no for an answer."

"Do you wish I had?" His light tone masked an underlying intentness.

"No," she replied softly. "You've made *my* life more interesting, too."

"This is only the beginning." He put an arm around her shoulders and hugged her to his side. "How about that drink? Let's throw caution to the winds."

Melissa hesitated. "I'm a little concerned about Betsy. We've been out all evening. Mrs. Flannery wouldn't have been able to get in touch with us if she needed me."

"I don't know why she would, but if it bothers you, we'll go home and check."

"Would you mind, Granger?" Melissa asked gratefully. "I just want to be sure Betsy is all right."

"No problem." He helped her into the car. "We'll have a drink at home instead."

* * *

Everything was quiet when they reached Granger's house. He went upstairs with Melissa to check on Betsy, who was in one of the guest rooms.

Moonlight streaming through the window illuminated the little girl curled up under the covers with Clancy asleep on the rug beside the bed. The dog awoke immediately and sprang up with a welcoming bark.

"Quiet, boy." Granger placed a hand gently around the pup's muzzle as Melissa bent over her sleeping daughter. "See? She's sleeping like a baby," he whispered.

They tiptoed out of the room with Clancy following them down the stairs.

After letting the dog out of the sliding glass door of the den, Granger crossed over to the bar. "What can I fix you to drink?"

"I really don't care for a drink," Melissa answered. "But you go ahead."

"Would you rather have coffee? Or better yet, let's have hot chocolate."

"That sounds good. We can stop somewhere on the way to my house."

"Why don't we make it here instead?"

"Are you allowed in the kitchen?" Melissa teased.

"Certainly—as long as Mrs. F. is asleep." He grinned.

The kitchen was sterile looking, but equipped with every modern appliance. Long countertops were covered with white ceramic tile that matched the immaculate white floor. All the cabinets were stained a dark walnut, which provided a rich contrast.

The effect was stunning yet austere. Melissa would have softened the room with flowering plants and perhaps gaily printed covers over the small appliances,

something to bring in a bit of color. This spotless sever-
ity would have depressed her on a daily basis, but it was
in keeping with Mrs. Flannery's personality. There was
no doubt that this was her domain.

Granger wasn't intimidated. He removed a carton of
milk from the refrigerator and rummaged through a
pantry for cocoa and sugar, disarranging cans and bottles heedlessly.

When the chocolate was hot they took their cups into
an adjoining breakfast room that was cozier than the
kitchen. It was furnished with a glass-topped table and
comfortable chairs. Although the seats were covered with
printed chintz, this room, too, would have benefited from
some plants.

Melissa mentioned the fact to Granger. "They'd do
beautifully in here. These windows overlooking the garden must let in a lot of sun."

"Okay. Bring in whatever you like," he said.

"I'd better not," she decided reluctantly. "Mrs. Flannery would have to water them regularly, and she probably doesn't want to be bothered."

Granger looked at her curiously. "She really intimi-
dates you, doesn't she?"

"I wouldn't say that. I understand how she feels about
this house, and I don't want to invade her territory. I
wouldn't want her messing around with my rose bushes."

He raised an eyebrow. "She rules over the inside, and
you rule over the outside. What's my function around
here?"

Melissa gazed at him through long lashes. "You're in-
dispensable."

"I'm glad you're starting to realize that," he murmured, leaning toward her.

"I do. You pay our salaries," she said mischievously.

"You set me up," he said disgustedly.

"Would I do a thing like that to you?" She laughed.

"Actually, I'm pleased." He lounged back in his chair and looked approvingly at her. "It means you're starting to relax with me. When you first came here, you were poised for flight every time I came close."

"Your reputation preceded you."

"I'm glad you're convinced that my intentions are honorable."

She slanted a glance at him. "I wouldn't go *that* far."

"Perhaps it was an overstatement." He chuckled. "But at least I'm honest about wanting to make love to you."

"You'd be disappointed," she said lightly. "My experience is very limited."

"We'd learn together." His voice deepened.

"Oh please, Granger! I might not believe everything that's written about you, but I do know you're no neophyte when it comes to making love."

"I don't pretend to be. I'm a mature man, not a high school boy." He curled a hand around the nape of her neck and drew her gently toward him. "What I meant was, you'd teach me what delights you the most, and I'd show you how much pleasure a man can give to a woman."

Melissa stared into his darkened eyes, feeling a spreading warmth ignite her midsection. She could imagine the ways Granger would arouse her. Every erogenous zone in her body cried out for his exploration.

His head descended toward hers, blotting out everything but desire. Her lips parted automatically for his kiss, welcoming the penetration of his tongue.

With a low sound of satisfaction, Granger scooped her into his lap without releasing her mouth. Melissa wound her arms around his neck, pressing tightly against him. Her entire body ached for the fulfillment he could bring.

"Sweet, passionate little Melissa." Granger buried his face in her hair. "You do want me, don't you, darling?"

"So much." She was beyond reason, driven by the passion he could always kindle.

"It's going to be so good, sweetheart," he crooned. "I'm going to make up for every disappointment you've ever suffered."

Granger's words chilled her. He wanted her, too, that was undeniable. But mixed with his desire was pity! Melissa couldn't accept that. Granger was a decent, caring man. He would make this a night to remember, but that wasn't enough. She didn't want his compassion—she wanted his love. The revelation shocked her. How had she allowed this to happen? She'd fallen in love with Granger!

When he cradled her against him and stood up, she struggled out of his arms. "It's getting late," she mumbled. "I have to go home."

After a moment's surprise he urged her face toward him. "What happened, Melissa?"

She refused to look at him. "Nothing happened. I'm just tired."

"Why are you so afraid to let me get close to you?" he asked gently.

"I didn't intend to let you get *that* close."

"Not consciously, perhaps, but when your instincts took over, you followed them. Doesn't that tell you something?"

"It tells me it's time to go home."

"You can't keep denying your emotions," he said softly. "You're a warm, passionate woman. Why is that so hard to accept?"

"I can take a cab," she said evenly.

"You know that won't be necessary. I'll take you home, if that's what you want."

Melissa hesitated. "Maybe I should take Betsy with me."

"Don't you think you're overreacting just a trifle? It was only a kiss."

"It has nothing to do with that," she said self-consciously. "I...uh...I always have a lot of errands to do on Saturday morning."

"Then it would be easier to leave Betsy here while you do them."

"They take quite a while. I might not be able to come back for her until noon or later." She was dredging up excuses desperately.

"I don't want to pressure you," he said quietly. "The decision is yours, naturally. I just hate to see you wake the child in the middle of the night."

Melissa knew Granger was the one making sense. She was being irrational in her desire to distance herself from him. But what good would it do? She'd have to be back here on Monday anyway.

She took a deep breath. "You're right, of course. I was simply trying to make things easier for everyone."

"I wish I could do the same." Before she could react to the compassion in his voice, he led the way to the front hall.

Granger had a gift Melissa envied. He could switch off his emotions and act perfectly natural after their brushes with intimacy. On the drive to her apartment he kept up a flow of casual conversation, discussing the movie they'd seen and how much he'd enjoyed the little Italian restaurant among other things. When they reached her house and Melissa tensed, preparing excuses if Granger suggested coming in, he set her mind at rest.

"Take all the time you need tomorrow," he told her pleasantly as they stood at her front door. "I'll keep Betsy happy."

"I shouldn't be too late," she mumbled.

"No problem." He leaned down and kissed her cheek. "Get a good night's sleep."

That was a laugh, Melissa thought as she went into the bedroom to get undressed after he left. How could she sleep when Granger had destroyed her nice, orderly life? Not that it was his fault, but that didn't make the circumstances any easier.

How could she go on seeing him without losing control of the situation? Because Granger wasn't going to give up easily. He knew their desire was mutual, so he couldn't see any reason not to fulfill it. If he ever found out she was in love with him, she'd be even more vulnerable.

The ideal solution would be to stop seeing him, but that presented as many problems as it solved. Besides the fact that she needed the money Granger paid her, there was Betsy to consider. She adored him. He was the first positive male figure she'd ever known. How could Melissa tell her she couldn't see him anymore? And then there was Clancy. Betsy firmly believed the dog was half hers. Would a seven-year-old child understand the games adults played?

Granger hadn't thought about the complications that might arise from his generosity. Or was it a calculated act? No, that couldn't be. She and Betsy weren't that important to him.

Melissa climbed wearily into bed. She almost hoped Granger would find someone else to concentrate on. At least then he'd be beyond her reach, no longer an almost unbearable temptation.

Chapter Seven

Melissa spent the restless night she'd predicted for herself. Dawn was starting to seep through the closed bedroom drapes when she finally fell asleep. Then sheer exhaustion took over.

It was noon by the time she showered, threw on her clothes and rushed over to Granger's house. He and Betsy were having lunch in the breakfast room, with Clancy waiting alertly for handouts.

"You're just in time for lunch." Granger greeted her with a smile.

"Mac and I went swimming this morning," Betsy informed her. "And this afternoon he's going to teach me to play Ping-Pong."

"Perhaps some other time. You don't want to wear out your welcome," Melissa said.

"I didn't ask him. It was Mac's idea."

As Betsy gave him a pleading look, Granger said to Melissa, "Have some lunch, and then you can decide what you want to do." Without giving her a chance to decline, he called to Mrs. Flannery, "Will you bring another place setting? Miss Fairfield is joining us for lunch."

Since she had to wait for Betsy to finish eating anyway, Melissa gave in without argument. Mrs. Flannery appeared in due time and silently set another place at the table.

"I want to thank you for taking care of Betsy," Melissa said to her. "I hope she wasn't any trouble."

"Mac *said* Clancy could sleep with me." Betsy spoke up quickly before the woman could answer.

Melissa gathered from the housekeeper's dour expression that there had been a conflict. "Mac has to learn to say no," she remarked grimly.

"*You* can teach me that." He grinned mischievously, passing her a bowl of salad.

Betsy was so eager to stay that Melissa didn't have the heart to refuse her. Secretly she didn't want to. Her pulse rate had sped up the minute she saw Granger. How could any man look that good in cutoffs and a T-shirt?

After lunch Granger took Betsy outside while Melissa remained behind to clear the table. It seemed only right, since she and Betsy weren't exactly guests.

"That was a delicious lunch," Melissa commented as she carried plates to the kitchen sink. "You're a wonderful cook, Mrs. Flannery."

"I try to do my job," the housekeeper answered without expression.

"Granger is lucky to have you," Melissa answered.

"*I* call him Mr. McMasters. I think an employee should know her place."

"Meaning me, of course," Melissa said directly. There was no point in avoiding the issue. Perhaps bringing it out into the open would clear the air between them.

"If the shoe fits," the older woman muttered.

"People are more informal nowadays," Melissa explained patiently. "The line between employer and employee isn't as rigid. I regard Granger as a friend."

"Is *that* what you call it?" Mrs. Flannery's lip curled.

Melissa's blue eyes started to smolder. "Exactly what are you implying?"

"You're pretty clever the way you've wormed your way in here. Don't think I haven't seen how you've been making up to the mister, parading around in tight clothes to get his attention."

"I wear jeans and a T-shirt to work, for Pete's sake!"

"If you ask me, precious little work gets done around here. Hanky-panky is what *I'd* call it."

Melissa tried to hang on to her rising temper. "That accusation is completely groundless. I do a job here the same as you do."

"Is that what you were doing last night?"

Melissa's cheeks bloomed as she remembered Granger's kiss and the way he'd cradled her on his lap. How could Mrs. Flannery have known about that heated incident?

"I know you were here last night," the woman said triumphantly, as though reading her thoughts. "You made a big enough mess in my kitchen."

Melissa breathed a sigh of relief. "We stopped by to check on Betsy, and then Granger made hot chocolate. After that he took me home. That's *all* that happened."

"You expect me to believe that?"

"I don't give a damn whether you do or not," Melissa answered succinctly. "I'm sorry you don't approve of me, but that's not going to change anything. I enjoy Granger's company, and I value his friendship."

"You're feeling mighty proud of yourself right now because you think you have him wrapped around your little finger, but I can tell you it won't last long. I've seen Mr. McMasters get interested in a woman before." The housekeeper laughed harshly. "One woman? Make that dozens of them. He acts the same way every time. Can't get enough of them at first, and then he loses interest. Just you wait and see. It will happen to you."

Melissa felt a stab of pain at hearing her private conclusions put into words. She lifted her chin, however, and stared regally at the housekeeper. "Considering how closely you monitor your employer's affairs, I'm surprised you get any work done." Without waiting for a reply, she left the room.

Granger and Betsy were playing Ping-Pong at a table he'd set up on the lawn between the pool and patio. The game was halted regularly, though, because Clancy would run off with the ball whenever it bounced off the table. Granger was laughing as the little girl chased after the dog.

"Where have you been?" he called when he caught sight of Melissa. "Betsy wants to show you how good she's getting."

"At chasing Clancy?" Melissa's nerves were still jangling after the unpleasant encounter with Mrs. Flannery.

"He does add a new dimension to the game." Granger chuckled. "How about a fast set while Betsy keeps him occupied?" He took another Ping-Pong ball out of his pocket.

"Thanks, but I really think we should leave."

He looked at her with a slight frown. "Is something wrong, Melissa?"

Was it that obvious? "No, of course not," she answered swiftly.

"You look flushed." He put the back of his hand on her cheek.

She jerked away, then felt self-conscious about over-reacting to his touch. "It's awfully warm today," she mumbled.

"I'll put a chair in the shade for you."

Before she could stop him, Granger went to bring one of the chairs from the pool area. While he was getting it, Betsy returned with Clancy at her heels.

"Will you hold his collar, Mom?" she asked plaintively. "Mac and I can't play if he keeps running off with the ball."

After they'd gone back to their game, Melissa stroked the dog's silky coat. "Poor Clancy. Neither of us is too popular around here today."

Mrs. Flannery's cutting words rang in her ears as Melissa gazed pensively at Granger. *He acts the same way every time...and then he loses interest.* If Melissa had dared to hope, she didn't any longer. Who would know better than his housekeeper?

Granger finally called a halt, over Betsy's protests. "This isn't much fun for your mother," he said. "Why don't you play with Clancy for a while?"

"Okay. Can we go swimming again later?"

"If it's all right with your mom." Granger walked over and sat on the grass at Melissa's feet. "Are you cooler now?" he asked.

"Yes, it's lovely in the shade." She looked up speculatively. "I wonder if those branches should be thinned out, though. This kind of tree needs good air circulation."

"It's your day off, remember?"

"How can I?" She smiled. "I'm at your house more than my own lately."

"I like that arrangement," he said softly. "I should feel guilty about taking up all your time, but I don't."

"You have nothing to feel guilty about. My free time isn't usually this glamorous. I'll be spoiled for any normal kind of life when I leave here." Melissa was careful to keep her tone light.

"The answer is simple. Don't leave me."

Granger's training as an actor almost made him sound as if he meant it. "Nothing is forever," she said evenly.

A curtain dropped behind his eyes and he lounged back on the grass. "I'm not asking for a guarantee. I know how you feel about long-term commitments."

How *she* felt! "People come and go," she said carelessly. "Except perhaps for Mrs. Flannery. She'll always be here."

"It's comforting to know I have at least one faithful woman in my life," he remarked dryly.

"And she can cook, too. How lucky can you get?"

"I'm the man who has everything, all right," he agreed, gazing at Melissa impassively. "Except a date for tonight. How about another movie?"

"I can't. Vivian doesn't get off night duty until Monday."

"That isn't a problem. Everything worked out fine last night. Betsy can simply spend the weekend here."

"No," Melissa said firmly. "She has to get back on her regular routine."

"Why? It's Saturday night."

"That doesn't mean she can stay up until all hours and eat a lot of junk."

"You just got through telling me Mrs. Flannery is a great cook."

"That's beside the point," Melissa insisted. "I want her at home tonight."

"Why?" Granger repeated.

"Because I said so! I'm beginning to feel as if I'm arguing with my daughter," she exclaimed in exasperation.

"Your edicts won't work with me. I'm not a seven-year-old." He smiled. "Maybe a movie doesn't appeal to you. What else can I offer to tempt you?"

As she gazed at his handsome, laughing face, Melissa could think of a number of things. It was fortunate that Mrs. Flannery made it impossible to accept his invitation.

Their discussion was cut short when Betsy raced over to them. The little girl's cheeks were flushed, and the dog was panting. "Clancy is thirsty, and so am I," she announced.

"Is his water bowl empty?" Granger asked.

"I don't know where it is."

"I'll show you." He stood up, saying to Melissa, "Ask Mrs. Flannery to bring out a pitcher of lemonade."

Melissa hesitated. "She might still be cleaning up the kitchen. Why don't I get some cans of soda out of the refrigerator in the bar?"

"Whatever you like." Granger motioned to Betsy to follow him.

Melissa went into the house. She was putting glasses on a tray when the telephone on the bar rang. Without thinking, she picked up the receiver and said hello. A click on the line told her she'd usurped one of Mrs.

Flannery's duties, another black mark against her, but it was too late to do anything about it.

"May I speak to Mac, please," a husky female voice asked.

"He's outside in the garden. Who's calling?"

Melissa knew she had no right to ask, but nothing could have stopped her. The woman was obviously someone who knew Granger well. Besides have his unlisted number, she called him Mac. He said that's what his good friends called him—which told Melissa where *she* stood. Granger had never suggested she use his nickname.

"Tell him it's Chloe," the woman answered. "I'll wait while you go and get him."

That was the name of the woman who had called during her first date with Granger. She seemed very certain he'd take her call, Melissa reflected as she went outside. Chloe wasn't mistaken. Granger started toward the house immediately when she delivered the message.

Melissa followed him inside. For a perfectly legitimate reason, she told herself. Granger had asked her to get the soft drinks.

His voice was vibrant as he picked up the phone. "Chloe, dear, how nice to hear from you. How's everything going?" After a pause he asked, "What can I do to help?" Her answer brought a gentle reproof. "Don't ever say that. You know I'm always here for you."

Melissa had heard more than she cared to. She picked up the tray of sodas and started for the sliding door. Granger didn't even glance up as she passed by. He was completely engrossed in his conversation.

"You worry too much, honey," he was saying soothingly. "You need to get out and have some fun."

Melissa stepped onto the patio and closed the glass door behind her.

Granger was on the phone for quite a while. When he finally joined them, Betsy asked if they could go swimming.

"It's all right with me." He looked questioningly at Melissa.

She couldn't very well say no. Granger would think she was miffed over his phone call. There was a limit to her endurance, however.

"You can swim for half an hour, and then we're leaving," she told Betsy firmly.

While they were changing in the cabana, Betsy said, "I'm having a really neat time. Mac is sure nice. I like him a lot."

"I'm not surprised," Melissa observed dryly. "He lets you do whatever you want."

"Not all the time. Last night he told me I couldn't have two desserts because I might get sick."

"It's nice to hear he isn't a complete pushover. How was your dinner?" Melissa asked casually.

"It was okay, but I don't like Mrs. Flannery."

"That's not very kind. She cooked dinner for you and took care of you last night. Wasn't that nice of her?"

"I guess so. But she always acts like she's mad about something, and she yells at Clancy."

"She isn't used to all the commotion you two make."

"We didn't spill anything last night," Betsy said defensively. "And that other time it was *her* fault."

"Well, don't worry about it. You won't be staying here again."

"I *like* staying here. I just don't like *her*."

"She comes with the territory," Melissa said crisply.

Betsy had lost interest in the subject. "I'm all ready. Can I go outside?"

"Yes, but don't go in the pool if Mac isn't there."

Although Granger must have realized that Melissa heard part of his phone call, he didn't refer to it. Nor did he try to change her mind about going out with him that evening. Obviously he'd made a date with Chloe. Melissa tried to match a face to the woman's sexy voice, then gave it up as an exercise in futility. She was someone glamorous. But unlike Felicia Grant, this woman was important to Granger.

Melissa went to Granger's house on Monday morning, not knowing what to expect. The fact that he hadn't called all day Sunday didn't necessarily mean he'd been with Chloe, but Melissa had a feeling they'd spent the weekend together. The question was, where? She steeled herself against seeing them come out of the house arm in arm.

Granger greeted her alone, however, looking well rested. As if he'd spent a lot of time in bed, Melissa thought bitterly.

"Did you have a nice weekend?" he asked pleasantly.

"Not as good as yours." She couldn't help herself.

He raised an eyebrow, but didn't pursue the subject. "I'm afraid Clancy dug up some of your plants."

"They're *your* plants."

"I like to think of them as ours. They were a joint effort."

When Granger gave her that warm, charismatic smile, Melissa always melted. "Well, I guess it isn't the end of the world. We can always get more plants."

"That's the right spirit," he said approvingly. "I'm glad to see you're not taking everything so seriously anymore."

"What's the use?" she sighed. "I can't change anything."

"What would you like to change?"

She gazed up at him, achingly aware of every virile inch of his splendid body. Glancing away quickly she said, "I'd like to do something about the pool house. I've been giving it some thought, and I believe hanging baskets of fuchsias would be very colorful. Come with me and see what you think."

"Whatever you decide is fine with me," he assured her, but he followed along obediently.

When they reached the cabana she told him to stand in the doorway. "I want to be sure someone your size won't bump his head."

"How far down do they hang?"

"That's what I have to decide." She glanced inside the room. "Is there a stool of some sort in here?"

"What do you need it for?"

"I want to measure from the top of the opening. A piece of string will give me a rough estimate." She took a twist of twine out of her pocket. "Now all I need is a stool."

"Here, I'll raise you up."

Granger put his arms around her hips and lifted her. As she reached above her head, her T-shirt pulled out of her jeans, exposing bare skin roughly on a level with his mouth.

He took advantage of the opportunity and kissed her stomach. "Did anyone ever tell you that you have a gorgeous belly button?"

"Stop it, Granger!" she ordered sharply. "Put me down."

"Not when I finally have you where I want you." He touched the tip of his tongue to the small depression.

"This isn't funny," she warned.

The words were stern, but her shaking voice undermined the effect. Melissa's entire midsection was on fire from his erotic caress.

"Mmm, you smell wonderful." He nuzzled her taut stomach. "What are you wearing?"

"Nothing right there! Will you kindly stop?"

"You don't really want me to," he murmured. "Why won't you admit it?"

The very thought panicked her. Melissa's only defense was righteous anger. "Wasn't your weekend with Chloe enough for you?" How dare he think he could go from one of them to the other?

Granger paused and looked up at her. "What do you know about Chloe?"

"I answered the phone when she called, remember?"

He finally lowered her to the ground. "That's right. I forgot."

"I'm not surprised," Melissa replied scathingly. "She had your full attention."

"So that's why you were so snippy with me this morning," he said softly.

"She had nothing to do with it—and I wasn't snippy!"

He smiled. "Let me tell you about Chloe."

"I'm not interested in hearing about her."

"That's too bad, because I'm going to tell you."

Before Melissa knew what he intended, Granger scooped her up and carried her into the pool house. Over her loud protests, he settled on the couch, holding her firmly in his arms.

"Chloe is a lovely lady," he began. "You two have a lot in common."

"I doubt that very seriously." Melissa tried to struggle free, without result.

"She's also raising a child by herself," he continued, ignoring the interruption. "Her son, Mark, is fourteen, an age when a child—especially a boy—needs a firm hand. He's a good kid, but he's starting to test her, to see what he can get away with. Chloe worries about him a lot."

"Did *his* father fade into the woodwork, too?" Melissa asked disgustedly.

"No, he was killed in a car crash."

"Oh. That's too bad."

Granger nodded. "Tony was my stand-in, and also a close friend. I've tried to do what I could for Chloe and Mark. Nobody can ever take Tony's place, but Mark needs a male authority figure at this stage. I straighten him out when he gets too rambunctious for his mother to handle."

The snatches of conversation Melissa had overheard took on a whole new context. The part about being there for Chloe when she needed him. "You really are a good friend."

"Isn't that what it's all about? People helping each other."

"Not everyone is as generous as you," she said softly.

"Does that mean I'm back in your good graces?" He laughed. "I don't even know what I did to land in the doghouse."

"Where is Clancy?" Melissa was glad for the diversion.

"At the groomers, and don't change the subject. You were spoiling for an argument when you arrived this morning. Why? What did I do between Saturday afternoon and Monday morning?"

"I wouldn't know." She couldn't look at him.

He tilted her chin up. "You thought I spent the weekend with Chloe."

"It was a natural assumption," Melissa said defensively. "After she called, you lost interest in me. I knew you'd made a date with *her*."

"I've never lost interest in you, but we'll get back to that. Why would it bother you if I did make a date with Chloe, since you'd already turned me down?"

"That wasn't what annoyed me." Melissa knew her earlier crankiness demanded some explanation. "I guess I was a little miffed that you don't consider me a friend."

"What gave you that idea?"

"Chloe and all your other close friends call you Mac. You never told *me* to."

"That's because you're special." His fingertips trailed down her cheek. "I'm hoping you'll call me something more intimate—like darling."

"I'm serious, Granger," she said weakly.

"So am I." He kissed her, slowly and savoringly.

Melissa couldn't summon the will to turn her head away. Granger's mouth was too seductive. It promised pleasure he was already delivering. His hand slipped under her T-shirt to caress her stomach suggestively.

"You have skin like warm satin," he murmured. "I want to touch all of you."

When his hand glided up to cup her breast, Melissa drew in her breath sharply. If she didn't stop him now it would be too late. She grasped his wrist, but when his fingers slipped inside her bra to stroke her sensitive nipple, she uttered a little moan of appreciation. The sensation was irresistible.

She relaxed in his arms as Granger strung a line of tiny kisses over her closed eyelids. "That's right, my love, just let it happen," he crooned.

Melissa was beyond protest when he stripped off her T-shirt and removed her bra. How often could she pull back from the brink? She quivered as he lowered his head to kiss her breasts, especially when his tongue curled around each coral peak.

"That feels so..." Words failed her as she dug her fingers into his shoulders.

He placed her gently on the couch and unsnapped her jeans. "I want it to be wonderful for you, darling."

"It already is," she answered in a breathy voice, offering no resistance when he removed the rest of her clothes.

Granger's eyes glowed as he stared at her nude body. "You're absolute perfection," he said huskily. When her lashes drooped under his avid inspection he cupped her chin in his palm and kissed her gently. "Don't be shy with me, angel. I want to know everything about you."

He stroked her body from shoulder to thigh, sending shock waves of desire rocketing through her. The sensual exploration was almost unbearably arousing. She arched her back and murmured his name over and over as his mouth traveled the path his hands had blazed.

"I want you so," she whispered.

"Do you know how long I've waited to hear you say that?"

Her appeal galvanized him. He stripped off his clothes in a blur of motion and stretched out beside her. Taking her in his arms he wound one leg around both of hers, welding the length of their bodies together. His mouth sought hers hungrily while his hands roamed restlessly down her back.

Melissa caressed him in the same way. All of her inhibitions vanished in the pure joy of gliding her palms over his smooth skin. Finally she grasped his buttocks in both hands and urged his hips against hers.

"You don't know what you're doing to me," he groaned.

Granger covered her body with his and parted her legs. Plunging deeply, he completed their union. The long-awaited reality was even more mind spinning than she could have imagined. Melissa rose to meet his thrusts, rocking against him as fevered pleasure escalated to incredible rapture.

The storm raged through them, growing in intensity until their muscles were strained to the limit. A final, powerful burst brought release. Their taut bodies relaxed as they spiraled down from the heights in shared fulfillment.

Neither stirred for long minutes. Finally Granger stroked her hair languidly. "You're slightly sensational, do you know that?"

Melissa turned her head to look at him searchingly. "Do you really mean it?"

"Couldn't you tell?"

"Well...I realize the women you've known have been a lot more experienced."

He kissed her with deep emotion. "I can truthfully say it's never been like this before."

"For me, too. I didn't even know it *could* be like this." Her voice held wonder.

"Today is only the beginning, angel. I'm going to make love to you a hundred different ways."

"I hope so," she said wistfully.

"Can you doubt it?"

She clasped her arms around his neck and snuggled closer. "I'm not asking for a commitment."

That would surely drive him away. But no matter what heartbreak she'd suffer when Granger's interest flagged, Melissa couldn't be sorry she'd followed her heart. Today was worth it!

He was looking at her without expression. "At least I managed to make one small chink in your armor."

"I don't have any defenses against you," she answered softly.

Granger's coolness vanished. "You don't need any, sweetheart. I promise I'll never hurt you."

"I know. You're kind to everybody."

"That sounds so impersonal. I was referring to *you*. Don't you know what you mean to me?"

"You're a wonderful person, Granger," she replied evasively. "I've never met anyone like you."

"That doesn't answer my question."

Melissa realized he was going to persist until he got an acceptable response. "I think you're fond of me," she said hesitantly. "It can't be just sex, because you could have women a lot more glamorous."

"You have no idea how very special you are, do you? What more could any man ask for? You're bright and loyal and loving. You have the face of an angel and a body that would drive the devil wild." He lowered his head to kiss the little valley between her breasts. "You're the most glamorous woman I've ever known."

Melissa smiled, running a fingernail lightly down his spine. "I love hearing you say it, anyway."

Granger raised his head to look at her. "You don't believe me? I can see we need to have a long talk." He arched his back as her teasing little caress began to have an effect. "We'll talk later," he murmured, cupping his hand around her breast and lowering his head once more.

Their lovemaking was even more thrilling this time, if possible. He aroused her unbelievably with his hands, his mouth, his hard frame. Melissa moved frantically against him, her body taut with desire, knowing what ecstasy lay in store. When he finally brought her to blessed completion, she whispered his name over and over, like a benediction.

Throbbing passion was replaced by a glow of contentment that permeated their joined bodies. The experience they'd shared was sublime. No words could describe it; none were necessary.

Melissa finally stirred reluctantly. "I'd like to stay here like this all day."

"That's what I had in mind." Granger wrapped her closer.

"I can't. I have a flat of marigolds in the trunk of my car. They'll wilt if I don't take them out."

"I never liked marigolds anyway."

"You probably don't even know what they are." She laughed.

"And I couldn't care less." He kissed her throat. "I want you here with me."

"When do you expect me to get my work done?" she teased.

"We'll figure something out. From now on I plan to take up all your time—starting with tomorrow night. I have to go to an awards dinner at the Century Plaza, and I want you to go with me." Before she had a chance to refuse, he continued, "And don't tell me you can't get a sitter. You must know by now that I wouldn't suggest calling an agency unless I thought they were reliable."

"That's no problem," Melissa said hastily. "Vivian is on days this week."

"But she won't be next week. We have to settle this thing. You really must let Betsy grow up, honey."

"That isn't the reason I haven't wanted to call an agency."

"Then what is?"

"I can't afford it," she mumbled.

He stared at her incredulously. "I don't believe this! You let me think you simply didn't want to go out with me all those nights? You must have known I'd gladly have paid for a sitter."

"You don't have to when you take out other women," she said defensively.

"What difference does that make? Besides, you aren't like any other woman in the world." His arms closed around her and his tongue traced the line of her closed lips seductively.

"The marigolds are drooping," Melissa said tentatively.

"What do you want to do about it?" He nibbled on her earlobe.

"They're hardy little devils. They can wait." She smiled enchantingly.

Vivian stopped by that day on her way home from work. "I haven't seen you all week," she commented as she sat at the kitchen table and watched Melissa prepare dinner. "Give me an update. How are you making out with the dreamboat of the Western world?"

"I'm still working for him, if that's what you mean," Melissa answered.

"You know it isn't. Tell me the good stuff. Did Granger ask you out again?"

"As a matter of fact he did," Melissa answered casually. "I was going to call and ask if you could baby-sit tomorrow night. Please say no if it's inconvenient. I feel guilty about asking you so often."

"I'm glad to do it. I've been urging you to go out. I never thought you'd hit the jackpot, though."

"I haven't." Melissa turned toward the sink. "Granger and I are just friends."

"Maybe now, but you never know what might develop."

"Can you really see Granger McMasters falling in love with me?" Melissa asked soberly.

"Why not? You're a knockout—even without the fancy clothes and jewelry your competition has."

"Thanks for the vote of confidence," Melissa said wryly. "You just put your finger on one of my problems. Granger is taking me to an awards dinner tomorrow night, and you've seen how glitzy those affairs are. I don't have anything to wear."

"That's an old cliché. You must have *something*."

"Believe me, I don't. I might squeak by in a little black dress if I was with an ordinary date, but Granger attracts so much attention. Everybody will be looking to see who he's with." Melissa chewed on her lower lip. "I don't want to be an embarrassment. Maybe I'd better tell him I can't go."

"You'll do no such thing! I have a closet full of clothes I've barely worn. You know what a compulsive shopper I am. Of course they're all too big for you, but we can take one in."

"You wouldn't mind?"

"I think it's a real hoot. My gown will get to go out with a movie star even if I never do. Come over after dinner and take your pick."

"You're a true friend. I don't know how to thank you."

"That's easy." Vivian grinned. "Find me a guy just like Granger."

"There's *nobody* like him," Melissa said softly.

Chapter Eight

Melissa chose the most subdued thing in Vivian's closet for her date with Granger—a forest-green satin dress. The full skirt was very short, but the close-fitting bodice had long sleeves and a demure neckline.

"With your figure you look sensational in anything." Vivian gazed enviously at Melissa's tiny waist. "But I still say you should have picked the red crepe. You'd really have stood out in the crowd in that number."

"I don't want to attract attention. It makes me uncomfortable to have people stare at me."

"You have to expect that when you're with Granger. Anyone he dates is news." Vivian held out a pair of pumps dyed to match the dress. "It's lucky we wear the same size shoes. Wouldn't you know the only thing dainty about me is my feet?" she asked disgustedly.

"Stop putting yourself down," Melissa said. "You have plenty of dates."

"Want to trade?" Vivian grinned. "I'll swap you two interns and a used-car salesman for Granger."

When the doorbell rang, Vivian hurried to answer it while Melissa filled her evening bag and sprayed herself with perfume.

Vivian had gotten over her awe of Granger, but she was hanging on his words when Melissa appeared. He glanced up and reacted in a most satisfactory way.

"You look beautiful—as always," he added.

"Any compliments should go to Vivian." Melissa laughed. "Almost everything I'm wearing belongs to her."

"You didn't have to tell him that," Vivian murmured.

Granger gave Melissa a smile that made her toes curl. "We don't have any secrets from each other," he said in a voice like lush velvet.

When they were in the car, Melissa scolded him mildly. "You'll really have to restrain yourself in front of Vivian. She already suspects we're a little more than friends."

"I don't care who knows it. I'd like to tell the world how lucky I am."

He drew her into his arms and kissed her deeply. Melissa responded instantly, pressing closely against him. Granger could arouse her with a glance; his touch was irresistible.

"I'm tempted to forget about the dinner and carry you off to bed instead," he groaned, caressing her body.

"I wouldn't complain," she whispered.

"I can't be that selfish."

"Force yourself," she teased.

"You're not making this any easier." He raised his head to give her a wry look. "I don't want you to think that's all I'm interested in."

"You're attracted to my agile mind?" she asked impishly.

He tilted her chin up and gazed at her with complete seriousness. "I'm attracted to everything about you, as any real man would be."

Melissa's throat felt tight. "I never knew there were men like you."

Granger smiled meltingly. "That's just as well. I wouldn't let any of them near you, anyway. Let's go to dinner. I want to show them what they're missing."

Klieg lights cut through the night sky as a long procession of limousines and expensive cars inched up to the entrance of the Century Plaza Hotel. Loud cheers from eager fans greeted the arrival of the more noteworthy personalities. It was a typical Hollywood production, complete with a red carpet rolled out to the curb and an emcee interviewing the most prominent guests. The cheers of the crowd intensified when a parking attendant opened their car door and Granger emerged.

The man with the microphone was alerted. He blocked their way as they started into the hotel, thrusting the mike in Granger's face. "Will you say a few words, Mr. McMasters? I understand your last picture broke records at the box office."

"It was very gratifying," Granger answered.

"Are you working on another picture?"

"Not at the moment. I'm enjoying a long-overdue vacation." Granger smiled charmingly. "Nice talking to you Barry."

The man wasn't about to let him get away that easily. "I don't believe I know your lovely companion," he said hastily. "Would you like to introduce her?"

"This is Melissa Fairfield." Granger put his arm around her waist and gazed into her wide eyes. "A very special friend."

The emcee stared at them avidly. "That sounds provocative. Do I detect romance in the air?"

Melissa held her breath, but Granger merely gave the man another smile. "If you'll excuse us, we have to find our table."

When they were safely inside, away from the microphone and television cameras, Melissa pointed out his indiscretion. "You shouldn't have said that. You know what people will say."

Granger shrugged. "They talk anyway. At least this time what they say will be true. You *are* a special friend."

She had to be satisfied with that. But her nagging disappointment vanished in the excitement of the glittering evening. Melissa was fascinated by all the designer gowns and the hordes of celebrities present. It was captivating to actually converse with famous stars.

After a long cocktail hour, dinner was served by a bevy of waiters wearing white gloves. The climax of the meal was flaming baked Alaska, and then the program began. Melissa enjoyed everything, even the acceptance speeches.

Unlike Granger. "I thought it would never end," he remarked several hours later as they drove away from the hotel.

"Really? I thought it was great fun. What didn't you like?"

"Wasting time when I could have been making love to you." He took her hand and lifted it to his lips.

"You had your chance," she teased.

"Can I have another one if I promise to be good?" he murmured.

Melissa's knees felt weak as she recalled just how good Granger could be.

He held on to her hand during the drive to his house. As they walked up the stairs to his bedroom, Melissa's anticipation mounted. When they were inside with the door closed, she turned to him eagerly.

Granger took her in his arms with a groan of satisfaction. "I couldn't have waited much longer."

They clung to each other, exchanging frantic little kisses and whispered endearments. After a few moments he slid her zipper to the waist and stroked her bare back.

"I love to touch you," he said huskily. "You're so smooth and warm."

Melissa's skin heated even more when he urged the dress off her shoulders and caressed her breasts. She drew in her breath sharply as his lips closed around one rosy tip. After he unclasped her belt, the dress slid to the floor, leaving her clad only in sheer pantyhose.

He rolled those slowly down her hips, pausing to string a line of provocative kisses over each newly exposed area of her body. Melissa trembled as his mouth slid over her stomach and his hands reached her thighs. She gasped when he placed a burning kiss at her most vulnerable point.

Sinking to the carpet, she clasped her arms around his neck. "Oh, Granger, you're driving me crazy," she moaned.

"Tell me what you want, sweetheart." He lifted her in his arms and carried her to the bed.

Her entire body throbbed as she watched him take off his clothes. Granger's hard chest, his lean hips and long muscular legs were as perfect as a classic sculpture. But Granger was unmistakably alive.

He flung his last garment aside and straddled her legs. "Tell me," he demanded again. "I want to hear you say it."

Melissa had no inhibitions left. She held out her arms and told him of her need.

His eyes glowed as he clasped her tightly and fused their bodies. The excitement built in intensity, escalating with every feverish movement, every rigid thrust. A final burst of ecstasy brought limitless peace.

They were both too content to move for a long time afterward. Melissa couldn't imagine anything more heavenly than falling asleep in Granger's arms. But when she felt herself drifting off, she stirred reluctantly.

"It must be late. I have to go home," she murmured.

"Not yet." His arms tightened.

"I can't keep Vivian up any longer."

"I suppose you're right." He sighed. "Okay, I'll take you home, but you'd better be prepared to make some changes. In the future you're going to call an agency for a sitter. I'll pay for it, and I don't want any arguments. Is that clear?"

Melissa looked over her shoulder at him mischievously as she prepared to get out of bed. "You're adorable when you put your foot down, do you know that?"

"You little devil." He pulled her back into his arms and caressed her intimately. "I'll teach you to make fun of me."

"No, Granger," she squealed. "I really have to go."

"Not until you promise to do as I say."

She stopped struggling and asked softly, "Have I ever denied you anything?"

He groaned and hugged her tightly. "How can I let you go?"

"There will be other nights," she whispered.

"It isn't enough. I want—" He stopped abruptly to look searchingly at her dreamy face. "I think we should have a talk, Melissa."

"Not now, darling. It's way past midnight. Cinderella has to go back to the real world."

Granger folded his arms behind his head and watched her gather up her clothes. "It's flattering to be cast in the role of Prince Charming."

"You're not only charming, you're extremely sexy." She grinned.

"Sort of like the icing on the cake," he remarked impassively. "Not vitally necessary, but an added enjoyment."

Melissa paused to look at him uncertainly. "Is something wrong, Granger?"

His expression remained set for a moment, then changed to an easy smile. "Nothing that couldn't be cured if you'd come back to bed."

The rumor mill didn't take long to start grinding. A picture of Melissa and Granger made the morning paper. The caption only said they were at the awards dinner, but a Hollywood gossip column went into more detail. It printed Granger's statement that Melissa was a special friend, then went on to speculate about the implication. Who was this mystery woman? Was she the superstar's new love interest?

Melissa confronted Granger with the item when she went to his house that morning. "I told you what would happen," she scolded.

He shrugged. "The gossipmongers make a big deal about every woman I take out. In a few weeks they'll tell the world I'm in love with someone else."

Melissa felt an actual pain in her chest. Even though she pretended to be annoyed at her sudden notoriety, she'd secretly hoped it might trigger a response from Granger. Some indication that he cared about her in more than just a physical way. His reaction told her how impossible that dream was.

She covered the hurt under an indifferent manner. "Have you picked her out yet?"

"Are you getting tired of me so soon?" he countered, his light tone belying the watchfulness in his eyes.

Melissa had already turned away. "It's more apt to be the other way around," she answered in a muted voice.

Granger drew her back against his chest and kissed the nape of her neck. "Dear heart, I can't imagine any man ever tiring of you."

He would, though. Mrs. Flannery's hurtful words came back to haunt Melissa once again. *At first he can't get enough of them, but it never lasts.*

She turned in Granger's embrace and put her arms around his waist. Her time wasn't up yet, and until then she was going to store up some precious memories.

The next couple of weeks were like a fairy tale. Granger took Melissa to nightclubs and elegant restaurants. He also took her to glamorous parties at fabulous estates where she met scores of celebrities.

But they also went to movies and ate in the little Italian restaurant he liked so much. And they made love at every opportunity, glorious, rapturous love that was new and exciting every time.

Melissa was in a perpetual state of radiance. Her life was as nearly perfect as it could possibly be. The idyl came to an abrupt end one fateful weekday afternoon, without any warning.

She was in the kitchen fixing an after-school snack for her daughter. When the doorbell rang, Betsy ran to answer it.

After a few moments she called, "Mom, come quick!"

Melissa raced out of the kitchen in response to the quavering note in the child's voice, then stopped in frozen dismay. Standing in the living room was a man with sandy hair and a handsome but weak face.

"He says he's my father," Betsy said uncertainly.

Melissa's body was taut as she stared at him. "What are you doing here?"

"Is that any way to greet the father of your child?" Stan asked.

Betsy pulled at her mother's hand. "Is he really my dad?"

"So I was led to believe." His smile was more of a smirk.

Melissa drew in her breath sharply. "What do you want?"

"To see my daughter. Is that so unnatural?"

She was at a disadvantage. If she voiced her true feelings, Betsy would find out what a rotten person her father really was. That was something Melissa had taken great pains to keep her from finding out.

"Come over here and sit on your daddy's lap," Stan said to Betsy.

She looked up at her mother doubtfully. "Do I have to?"

His face darkened as he glared at Melissa. "I see you've done a number on me."

"It's been a long time. She doesn't remember you," Melissa said hastily.

"Well, we'll just have to get reacquainted." He patted the cushion beside him on the couch. "Come sit next to me." When Betsy had obeyed gingerly he said, "Tell me about yourself. How old are you now?"

"I'm seven. Pretty soon I'll be eight, and then I'll be in the third grade."

"That's nice. I'll bet a beautiful little girl like you has lots of boyfriends."

"I'm too young yet, but Mom has a boyfriend," Betsy volunteered. "His name is Mac. Well, really his name is Granger, but he told me to call him Mac. That's what all his good friends call him," she said complacently.

"Why don't you go over to Cathy's and play for a while?" Melissa asked sharply.

Stan's hand fastened around the child's wrist. "We're just getting to know each other. Tell me more about Mac," he instructed Betsy.

She was happy to comply. "He takes us lots of places, and he buys me things. Mom says he's spoiling me, but he doesn't listen to her." Betsy gave her mother a gamin grin.

"It sounds as if you like him a lot," Stan remarked casually.

"Oh, I do! Mac even bought me a dog. Well, it's only half mine, but I get to go over to his house and play with it."

"That's a convenient arrangement." Stan smiled thinly. "I guess if I want you to visit *me* I'll have to buy a pet, too."

"Where do you live?" Betsy asked.

"Nowhere as grand as your friend Mac, but that's going to change. How about it? Would you like to stay with me for a few days?"

Before she could answer, Melissa asked ominously, "Exactly what are you up to?"

His expression was bland. "I'm trying to make up for lost time."

"It's too late for that!"

"It's never too late. Betsy and I are going to be great pals, aren't we, kid?" He put his arm around the little girl and squeezed her to his side. "We'll have to work out some kind of schedule," he told Melissa. "Maybe she can spend weekends with me."

"When hell freezes over," Melissa said through gritted teeth, no longer trying for restraint. "Stay away from my child!"

"She happens to be my child, too."

Betsy squirmed away from him, giving her mother an apprehensive look. "Can I go over to Cathy's now?"

"That's a good idea." Melissa forced a smile. "I'll be over to pick you up later." She waited until Betsy had run out the door before confronting Stan again. "Why have you come back after all these years? And try to tell the truth for once."

"You're being pretty hard on me," he complained. "Can't a man get lonesome for his wife and daughter?"

"*Ex*-wife, and you were never here even when we were married."

"Things are going to be different. From now on I plan to be around a lot."

"That sounds like a threat. You don't give a damn about Betsy, and you certainly don't care about me. What's in back of all this?"

"You're really bitter, aren't you?"

"I have a right to be. Not because you walked out on me—we had a rotten marriage. But you never contributed one thin dime toward Betsy's support."

"Yeah, I'm sorry about that. But I'll make it up to you."

"I don't need you anymore," Melissa said scornfully.

"So I read in the papers. You really hooked yourself a live one, didn't you?" His eyes crawled over her appraisingly.

She was suddenly wary. "I don't know what you're talking about."

"You don't have to keep up appearances with me. Betsy confirmed what I already knew—that you're Granger McMasters's girlfriend. A big movie star like that is really loaded."

Melissa's eyes glinted dangerously. "Are you intimating that Granger is keeping me?"

Stan glanced around. "Not on too grand a scale, but you probably know what you're doing. It takes time to reel in a fish that big."

"That's disgusting! For your information, I've never taken one cent from Granger."

"Then you're a fool," Stan said calmly. "You two aren't sitting around nights discussing good books. If you're giving it away free, you're not very smart."

Her nails bit into her damp palms. "Get out of my house, Stan."

He lounged back on the couch instead. "Don't lose your cool. We haven't discussed our daughter yet."

Melissa's eyes narrowed. "I can't believe you're serious about wanting to spend time with her. That's as phony as everything else about you. But just in case you think it might be amusing to play at being a father for a while, forget it. You gave up any right to Betsy when you deserted her."

"A judge might not be so unforgiving."

"Just try it and see how far you get," she answered furiously.

"Are you willing to take a chance?" he asked softly.

Fear suddenly twisted Melissa's insides at the very thought of going to court. She hadn't received much justice the last time around.

As though reading her thoughts, Stan said, "You never claimed I abused Betsy in any way. I'm sure a judge would order you to let me see my child."

"He'd also order you to pay the child support payments you owe."

"That could be worked out."

"We're not talking about small change. Did you inherit a gold mine?"

"Let's just say I have prospects."

Melissa wasn't interested, nor did she believe he was serious about turning over a new leaf. "Why don't you tell what you *really* want, Stan?"

"Well, now that it's come up, I *could* use a job."

She stared at him in bewilderment. "How can I help you? I don't even know what you do. Are you still a salesman?"

"Selling is penny ante stuff. I want to get into a field that pays big bucks. Like the entertainment industry," he added casually.

"What do you know about show business?"

"It's like everything else in life. It isn't *what* you know, it's *who* you know. Your friend Granger could get me a job just like that." Stan snapped his fingers.

"Doing what?"

"Any number of things. I'm willing to start out reasonably small—as long as it pays big. I have the know-how to work my way up, all I need is a foot in the door."

"Get real, Stan! You never succeeded at anything. Why would I ask Granger to get you a job?"

"Because one hand washes the other, baby. You do me a favor, and I'll overlook the fact that you're having a well-publicized affair with a notorious womanizer."

"Even if either of those things were true, it's none of your business. We're not married anymore."

"But we have a child to think of," he answered smoothly. "Some people might consider you an unfit mother. The court, for instance, if I brought it to their attention."

"Which you plan to do if I refuse to be blackmailed."

"You always did think the worst of me," he said reproachfully. "It would hurt me to have to take Betsy away from you. But we both know that doesn't have to happen."

She tried to control her rising panic. "What if Granger refuses to stick his neck out for you?"

"It's as much for you as it is for me, doll. You won't have any trouble making him see the light. I don't have to tell *you* how a woman gets what she wants out of a man."

Melissa didn't allow her revulsion to show. It was more important to find some way out of Stan's trap. "Suppose I talk Granger into getting you a job, and it doesn't work out? You don't have even basic movie experience. What happens then?"

"I'm not worried about cutting it. All you have to do is suck up to the right people. But hey, I'm realistic. The bigger the rewards, the more chance there is of getting stabbed in the back."

"Exactly," she said anxiously. "I've met these people. They'll chew you up and spit you out."

"Well, if your boyfriend can't protect me, I guess he'll just have to give me a stake so I can try some other line of work."

"I see. You expect me to be your meal ticket for the rest of your life," Melissa said bitterly. "This is only the beginning. Blackmail never stops, does it?"

"I prefer to think of it as extending a helping hand to your fellow man," he replied suavely.

"You aren't a man. You're pond scum!"

He wasn't upset by her invective. "If you feel that way, I guess it would bother you a lot to have me raise our child."

"You're bluffing! You wouldn't waste your time on her."

"Watch me." Stan's steely eyes clashed with Melissa's. Then his genial mask slipped back in place. "We won't get anywhere trading insults. Besides, it isn't as though I'm making outrageous demands. I think I'm being very understanding about this whole thing."

"You're one of a kind, all right." Her lip curled. "Not many men would think of selling their daughter."

Stan's patience showed signs of waning. "Don't hand me that holier-than-thou garbage. Your morals aren't precisely above reproach."

"I've done nothing to be ashamed of," Melissa answered tautly.

"You can tell that to the judge if we don't come to an agreement. I'll give you twenty-four hours to get your boyfriend's cooperation." He rose and looked her up and down insolently. "It should be a piece of cake. Now I remember why I married you."

"Get out before I throw you out," she said in a low, deadly tone of voice.

"You really should do something about that temper of yours." Stan sauntered to the door. "I'll see you tomorrow at this time, and you'd better have news I want to hear." He paused for effect. "Otherwise, our next meeting will be in court, doll face."

Melissa began to tremble uncontrollably after he left. Stan wasn't making idle threats. If she didn't do what he said, he would try to take Betsy away from her. Whether he could succeed or not didn't bear thinking about.

The telephone bell jangled Melissa's already raw nerves. She picked up the receiver with a shaking hand. Cathy's mother sounded ludicrously normal, as though the earth wasn't wobbling on its axis.

"It's Joyce Harrison," she said. "I'm calling to ask if Betsy can stay for dinner. The girls are in the middle of a game of Monopoly. If it's all right with you, I'll bring Betsy home right after dinner."

"Thanks, but you can phone me and I'll come and pick her up," Melissa said.

"It's no trouble," the woman assured her. "I have to go out, anyway."

Melissa was grateful for the respite. She couldn't have faced her daughter at that moment. Not with their lives hanging in ruins.

The phone rang again almost as soon as she put it down. This time it was Granger. "Hi, angel. I just called to say I might be a few minutes late."

Melissa gripped the phone. "I can't see you tonight, Granger."

"Why not? What's up?"

Hysteria threatened to overwhelm her. "I can't see you ever again. Please don't call me anymore."

"What's happened, Melissa?" he asked sharply.

She took a deep breath to calm herself. "It's a long story, and I can't go into it right now. If I mean anything at all to you, please leave me alone."

"Stay right where you are," he ordered. "I'll be over in a few minutes."

"Didn't you hear what—" But Granger had hung up.

Melissa paced the floor distractedly. It was too much to expect that he would accept her request without an explanation. Granger might even offer to meet Stan's terms when he found out, but that would only solve the problem temporarily. Stan would continue to make outrageous demands, using Betsy as a club.

Granger's car screeched to a stop in front of Melissa's house an incredibly short time later. He strode into the apartment, looking deeply concerned. "Tell me what this is all about. You couldn't have meant what you said on the phone."

"I didn't have any choice. It has to be that way."

She told him the whole story with deepening despair. Granger's face darkened as he listened. When she was finished, he swore pungently.

"I know," she said sadly. "Stan is all of that and more. He's the lowest form of life. Which is why I can't see you anymore."

"You're not thinking clearly, sweetheart. He already knows about our relationship. What good would it do for us to stop seeing each other?"

"I could tell him you turned me down. That you aren't interested in me any longer. He doesn't really want Betsy. Maybe he'll leave me alone if there's nothing in it for him."

"You think he'll believe I'd drop you without even talking to him?"

"It's possible." Melissa's fingers twisted together nervously.

"Blackmailers aren't gullible by nature."

"I don't know what else to do. I can't let him take Betsy!"

"He won't, darling," Granger soothed. "I'll get the best lawyers in town. They'll tear his credibility to shreds."

"You have a lot more faith in the judicial system than I do," she said bitterly.

"Trust me, angel. He doesn't have a leg to stand on."

"But that's the whole point. He does! All those pictures of us in the newspapers, and the articles in the tabloids. They've made our relationship sound so sleazy." Melissa ran shaking fingers through her long hair. "A judge might very well consider me an unfit mother. Especially if it's a male judge. Stan will come out looking like a choirboy by comparison."

"Do you want me to get him a job?" Granger asked quietly.

"You don't get rid of a rat by feeding him." She sighed.

"I'm willing to do anything you say, but you have to tell me," he said patiently. "If you don't want to fight, and you don't want to knuckle under, what *do* you plan to do?"

"I wish I knew," she said distractedly. "Maybe I should take Betsy and run. Stan managed to disappear for years."

"You aren't serious!"

"Why not? I could change our names, move to another town." Her eyes were a little wild. "We could go to some other state. He'd never find us."

Granger grasped her shoulders and gave her a little shake. "You're getting carried away, sweetheart. Stop and think about what that would mean. You'd have to teach Betsy to lie every time anyone asked her a personal question. You'd both have to be on your guard constantly. And if anyone got the least bit suspicious, you'd have to pull Betsy out of school and move on to the next town. Is that what you want for your daughter, to make her a fugitive?"

Melissa bowed her head. "It sounds so horrible, but anything would be better than letting Stan get his hands on her."

Granger gathered her into his arms. "I won't let that happen, I promise you."

"That's nothing anybody can do. He holds all the cards."

"Not all. I think I have a solution to your problems."

She raised her head to gaze at him earnestly. "Tell me. I'll do anything!"

"We could get married," Granger said, as casually as if he were suggesting a movie. "That would defuse his claim that you were having a tawdry affair."

"You mean, pretend to get married?" she faltered. "I don't know if Stan would buy that."

"I'm sure he'd demand to see a marriage certificate," Granger answered dryly. "What I'm proposing is the real thing."

"That wouldn't work, either. I'd have to move in with you to convince Stan, and then the media would find out. They're always on your trail."

He smiled. "I don't have any problem with our living together."

"I'm serious, Granger!"

"So am I. It's the perfect arrangement. You'll have security, and Betsy will get her own room and full possession of Clancy. I doubt if she'll put up any objections." He chuckled.

"What will you get out of it?"

His expression became guarded. "I like having you both around. You've added a new dimension to my life. I'm not willing to lose you and Betsy because of that jerk."

"But marriage means all kinds of commitments," she protested, gazing at him searchingly.

His eyes were unreadable. "Ours would be different. Our motivation might be unconventional, but perhaps it makes more sense than the reason people usually get married."

Because they fall in love, Melissa thought with a pang. Granger wasn't pretending love was involved.

"We're certainly compatible," he continued. "We enjoy each other's company, and the physical attraction between us is very strong. We're better suited than a lot of couples who marry for purely emotional reasons."

"Like expecting to spend the rest of their lives together?" she asked in a low voice.

"We wouldn't be bound by the same rules," he answered evenly. "Our marriage won't be a trap."

Could she enter into a loveless marriage, knowing Granger was only on loan to her? Someday he'd meet someone else and want his freedom. That would be unbearable. But if she accepted Granger's offer, Betsy would be safe. How could she possibly refuse?

Granger was watching her closely. "What's your decision. Shall we get married?"

"I guess so." She sighed.

His jaw set grimly. "If it's going to make you that unhappy, let's forget the whole thing."

"I didn't mean to sound ungrateful. You're being unbelievably kind. I'm just worried that you might regret your generosity when Betsy and I move in and start to cramp your life-style."

Granger's rigid jaw relaxed. "I expect some fringe benefits," he teased.

"I hope it's enough," she said hesitantly.

He framed her face in his palms and kissed her sweetly. "You're enough for any man. Sooner or later I'm going to convince you of that."

"If you ever change your mind, I'll give you a divorce," she said soberly. "I won't ever become a liability."

"You're a lot more generous than I am." He gathered her close and gazed at her in triumph. "You're going to belong to me completely, and I hang on to what's mine."

Chapter Nine

Melissa and Granger were discussing the wedding plans when Betsy returned home. The little girl's rather subdued face lit up when she saw Granger.

"We've been waiting for you," he said. "Your mom and I have something to talk to you about."

Apprehension returned to shadow the child's eyes. "Does it have anything to do with my dad?"

"Not really. Why would you think that?"

"He was here today. He and Mom got in a fight over me."

"It was just a slight disagreement," Melissa corrected her hastily.

"He wanted me to come and stay with him, and you said I couldn't."

Granger interceded. "Sometimes mothers have to say no to things that children want to do."

"I don't want to go with him," Betsy said quickly. "He isn't anything like I expected."

"What did you expect?" Granger asked cautiously.

"Somebody like you. We have fun together. He asked me dumb questions, and he squeezed me real hard. And when he talked to Mom, he had a funny look on his face. I don't think he really likes us very much."

"You can fool some of the people," Granger murmured. "I'm sure your father loves you," he told the child. "But you won't be staying with him. How would you feel about moving to my house? Your mother and I are going to get married. If that's all right with you."

"Do you really mean it?" Betsy threw her arms around his neck. "You're going to be my new dad?"

"You're not worried about having a wicked stepfather?"

She laughed delightedly. "I know you're teasing me. Can we move in right now?"

Stan didn't give up without a struggle. He made a nasty scene the next day, but this time Granger was present, a much more formidable adversary. After he pointed out why the blackmail scheme was no longer workable, Stan threatened to sell his story to the tabloids. They'd lap up his version of a poor, wronged father being denied even visitation rights with the daughter he adored.

Melissa was distraught at the thought of Betsy's name being dragged through the mud with the rest of them, but Granger took care of that threat with icy calm. He told Stan he'd hired a firm of private detectives in anticipation of just such a dirty trick. They were already digging into Stan's past. If they uncovered anything even faintly questionable, it would be turned over to the district attorney.

From the way Stan paled, Melissa realized his past couldn't stand scrutiny. He blustered and issued empty threats, but when Granger suggested he might prefer to leave town—in which case he would drop the investigation—Stan snarlingly agreed.

After he'd gone, Melissa hesitantly suggested to Granger that they no longer needed to get married. But he said they didn't actually know that any charges against Stan would stick. If they didn't go through with their original plan, she was still in a vulnerable position.

Melissa agreed, partly because she knew Granger was right, but partly because she couldn't bear to give him up.

The wedding was arranged in a week, but it was as lovely as if it had been planned for months. Melissa had expected to go down to City Hall and be married quietly by a justice of the peace, but Granger wouldn't hear of it.

He took care of all the details, flowers, caterer, the guest list. He even went with Melissa to pick out a wedding gown. She was in a daze of happiness—until he brought her back down to earth.

When she protested the lavishness of the preparations, Granger said, "I want to look back on my first wedding as something special."

In spite of her secret longing for their vows to be binding, Melissa was a radiant bride. Her gown was an exquisite creation of champagne-colored lace, and she carried a bouquet of white orchids tied with long streamers of champagne-colored ribbon. The ceremony took place in Granger's garden, under a canopy of fragrant flowers.

Melissa felt a sense of unreality as the minister spoke the solemn words that would change her life so drastically. Surely this was all a dream. But when Granger took her in his arms, she didn't want to wake up.

"My beautiful wife," he murmured. "We're going to be happy together, I promise."

"I already am," she whispered as his mouth covered hers.

They had only that brief moment together before the guests crowded around, offering congratulations. Betsy was exhilarated by all the excitement, and Vivian was dazzled. She and Betsy had been Melissa's attendants.

"I'm black and blue from pinching myself," Vivian declared. "It's like a fairy tale."

"I'm glad you approve." Granger smiled at her. "Let me get you a glass of champagne."

"Can I have some, too?" Betsy asked.

"Why don't you have ginger ale instead?" he suggested. "That's what I'm going to have."

"You aren't drinking?" Melissa asked.

He gave her a slow smile. "I don't want to blunt any of my senses."

When Melissa blushed like a schoolgirl, Vivian laughed. "Where are you going on your honeymoon?" she asked.

"We haven't decided yet," Granger answered.

"Nothing like waiting till the last minute. Your honeymoon started five minutes ago."

"We're going to postpone it for a while. Until Betsy gets accustomed to her new surroundings," he explained.

"She looks pretty happy to me," Vivian commented.

They all glanced over at the little girl who was flitting around the garden from one guest to another, her face alight.

Betsy wasn't the problem; Mrs. Flannery was. She was far from reconciled to Granger's marriage, although Melissa had tried to gloss over the bad feeling between them. Guessing that the housekeeper expected to be fired, she'd made a point of assuring her that her job was secure, which hadn't mollified the woman.

Mrs. Flannery was coldly polite to Melissa, and barely tolerant of Betsy. The chances of winning her over didn't seem great, but Melissa was determined to try. It seemed cruel to dismiss the woman after so many loyal years of service.

As dusk gathered, the garden became a fairyland of twinkling lights. Dozens of candles shielded by glass hurricane lamps were mounted on tall poles placed in the flower beds. More candles and floral arrangements graced the tables that were set up on the spacious lawns.

When darkness fell, a lavish buffet was set out on a long, linen-covered banquet table. The towering wedding cake was displayed on another table, surrounded by luscious-looking tarts, French pastries and fancy cookies.

Granger had thought of everything. During the afternoon a string quartet entertained softly. It was replaced after dinner by a group that played dance music.

Melissa and Granger had little time to talk privately. She followed him from group to group, feeling like a guest at his party. Reality didn't set in until the last well-wisher had straggled off and the caterers began to clean up. This was her home from now on. She and Granger were married!

The strangeness returned when they walked up the stairs to his bedroom. Melissa still thought of it as his, even though her clothes were hanging in the closet.

"I can't believe I'm going to stay all night." She laughed to cover her sudden constraint.

Granger took her in his arms. "Tonight and every night. You're a permanent part of my life from now on."

"I hope so," she whispered.

"Believe it, my love."

Melissa held her breath. That was the closest Granger had ever come to saying he loved her. Did he mean it, or was it just a term of endearment?

"You were an enchanting bride," he said huskily. "I couldn't take my eyes off you, and neither could anyone else."

She smiled diffidently. "It was this dress you bought me."

"That's only the beginning. You wouldn't let me buy you anything before, so I plan to make up for lost time. I'm going to dress you in silk and satin." His lips slid down her neck. "And then I'm going to *un*dress you."

"You don't have to buy me things. All I want is—"

He raised his head to look at her with gleaming eyes. "What do you want, darling? Tell me and it's yours."

Melissa's courage failed her. Love wasn't something you could ask for; it had to be offered. Granger had given her everything else. This was their wedding night and she wasn't going to do anything to spoil it.

"I want you to make love to me," she murmured.

"I'd consider it a privilege," he answered softly.

Granger removed her dress and gazed at her with something akin to reverence. Her body was slender and supple, clad in exquisite lingerie. He touched her wispy bra with his fingertips, then leaned forward and kissed the rosy nipple that peeped through the lace.

Melissa grasped his shoulders to steady herself as he touched the sensitive spot with his tongue. The sensation became even more erotic when his teeth gently tugged at the lacy fabric until one breast was exposed.

While his lips closed around the small rosette, he caressed her stomach and hips. She began to tremble when one forefinger slipped inside the waistband of her panties and began a slow exploration.

Throwing her arms around his neck, she pressed close to him. "How is it possible to want someone this much?" she gasped.

"Because we're made for each other, little angel."

Granger unclasped her bra and lifted her in his arms. As he carried her to the bed, she unbuttoned his shirt. He stood her on her feet briefly while he shed his clothes and removed her last garment. Then they moved into each other's arms, their bodies conforming perfectly, melting together with the heat of their desire.

"You're my other half," he muttered hoarsely. "The part I've been missing."

"I'm here now." Melissa swayed backward, taking him with her onto the bed.

His eyes were incandescent as he stared down at her passion-filled face. "And I'll never let you go."

Granger's possession was fierce, yet tender. He brought her ecstasy, and when the scorching need subsided to a warm glow, he fanned the embers and raised her to the heights again.

Their wedding night was all Melissa could have wished for and more, so much more. After the wonder of their lovemaking, they were both utterly content.

In the week that followed, Melissa felt as though she were living in paradise. Except for Mrs. Flannery, who showed no signs of unbending, life couldn't have been more perfect.

But marriage also changed Melissa's life in ways she hadn't anticipated. For one thing it came as a shock when Granger hired someone else to do the gardening. She realized that was only practical, but it made her a little uneasy.

"What am I going to do with myself every day?" she asked.

"I'll think of something." He gave her a sultry look.

She laughed helplessly. "We can't spend all of our time in bed."

"Can you think of anything better to do?" he asked in a throaty voice.

She could never resist him. Twining her arms around his neck, she said, "Give me a month or two to come up with something."

Melissa realized she had to develop her own interests, but that could come later. Right now she was content to spend every moment with Granger. After all, they were on their honeymoon.

It was an idyllic time. During the day they wandered through museums or drove to the beach or went shopping. Granger took Melissa to the famous-name boutiques on Rodeo Drive and insisted on outfitting her from head to toe.

He bought her dressy things and casual wear, cashmere sweaters in heavenly shades of lavender, periwinkle and creamy white, all with pants or skirts to match. He bought her shoes to go with every outfit, along with belts, blouses and lingerie.

"I don't even want to think about how much money you spent," she fretted as they drove home from yet another shopping spree.

"Then don't." He chuckled and reached over to take her hand. "When are you going to realize you have a rich husband?"

"I didn't marry you for your money," she answered soberly.

Granger's expression changed and he removed his hand. "I know why you married me." After a moment he asked, "How about a swim? Betsy should be home from school by now."

Melissa was able to put up with Mrs. Flannery's uncooperativeness, but she didn't know how to explain it to Betsy.

"She won't let me get milk and cookies when I come home from school," the little girl complained. "I can't even go in the refrigerator."

"Does that really matter so much? Mrs. Flannery puts them out for you on the breakfast room table," Melissa said placatingly. "She just prefers that you stay out of her kitchen. You must admit you make a mess sometimes."

"*You* never minded."

"She's a bit fussier. Mrs. Flannery likes to keep the house neat."

"It isn't her house. It's Mac's."

"We all live here together, and we have to try and get along."

"*He'd* let me eat wherever I wanted. I'm going to ask him to tell her I can."

"No, you're not," Melissa said swiftly. "We aren't going to bother Mac with anything that trivial."

"Then *you* tell her."

"All right." Melissa stifled a sigh. "I'll have a talk with her."

The conference wasn't a success. Mrs. Flannery refused to unbend, even though Melissa tried to be as diplomatic as possible.

"I realize this transition period is difficult for you," she told the woman. "We're all accustomed to doing things a certain way, but I'm sure we'll get used to each other's habits if we try." When the housekeeper merely gave her a stony stare, Melissa plowed on. "Betsy has always been allowed in the kitchen, and I'd appreciate it if you didn't make her feel unwelcome."

"What stories has she been telling you about me?" Mrs. Flannery demanded.

"I wouldn't put it that way. She simply doesn't understand why she can't get a glass of milk when she likes. In case you didn't realize it, Betsy doesn't need to ask my permission."

"I'm sure of *that!*"

Melissa ignored the muttered comment. "So I'd appreciate it if you'll be a little more flexible with her."

The housekeeper shrugged. "Whatever you say. But if Mr. McMasters complains because the house is going to seed, I don't intend to take the blame."

"I scarcely think a few crumbs on the kitchen floor will depreciate the property," Melissa answered dryly.

"Nothing's the same as it was before, what with toys all over the place and dog hairs on the furniture." The housekeeper's smoldering resentment burst forth. "I used to keep this house looking like a showplace."

"That's very admirable, but Mr. McMasters actually prefers a more lived-in look."

Mrs. Flannery's jaw set stubbornly. "He never made any complaints."

"I'm sure he didn't, but we're a family now. We all have to make adjustments. I'm asking for your cooperation."

"Do I have a choice?"

Melissa's teeth clicked together at the woman's insolence. "Slavery has been abolished," she said succinctly. "You can always quit."

Mrs. Flannery's face paled. "Are you firing me?"

"No, I merely pointed out the option if you find your working conditions intolerable."

"This is my home," the housekeeper said unsteadily. "I wouldn't know where to go."

Melissa's anger evaporated. "I'm not putting you out or trying to take your place," she said gently. "You're welcome to stay as long as you like. Just try to understand that the house isn't as important as the people in it. We aren't looking for perfection."

Mrs. Flannery nodded and turned away wordlessly.

Their talk produced a change in her attitude from then on. The older woman was just as distant, but at least now she masked her scorn and disapproval. She was expressionlessly polite to Melissa and tolerated Betsy with grim stoicism. All of her warmth was lavished on Granger.

Melissa wasn't happy with the situation; it was like living with a hostile robot. But she knew they were stuck with the woman. How could she turn out someone who was that alone? The fear in Mrs. Flannery's eyes had touched Melissa. She was also moved by her devotion to Granger. Under that uncompromising exterior was a heart, however unlikely it seemed.

Melissa and Granger had two perfect weeks together before reality intruded. One day while they were lazing by the pool, Granger got a phone call that ended their honeymoon.

"Damn!" he muttered when he returned from the den. "That was the studio. They want to reshoot some scenes in the last picture I did for them."

"You're going back to work?" Melissa asked.

"Only for a week. It shouldn't take any longer than that."

"Can I come with you one day? I've never been on a movie set."

"Well, that's the trouble, honey. I have to go back on location. The picture was shot in a remote part of Wyoming."

"You made a cowboy movie?"

"No, I play a millionaire playboy. I make a bet that I can survive in the wilds for a month, all alone in a shack."

"Do you win the bet?"

He smiled. "You don't want me to give away the plot, do you?"

"That's one of the advantages of being married to the star."

Granger came over to sit on the edge of her chaise. "Can you think of any other advantages?"

"A few that I'll miss while you're gone."

"You're not the only one," he groaned. "I'd take you with me, but you'd be terribly bored. The location site is out in the wilderness, miles away from civilization. You'd get tired of watching us shoot, and there wouldn't be anything else for you to do. When I get back we'll plan a real vacation," he promised. "We haven't had our honeymoon yet."

She stroked his cheek lovingly. "What do you call this?"

"A little slice of paradise." He turned his head and kissed her palm. "But I want to take you someplace exotic. How about a cruise through the South Seas? Or maybe you'd prefer to rent a chalet in Switzerland?"

"Those sound like extended trips," Melissa said doubtfully.

"We have all the time in the world."

"I couldn't leave Betsy for any long period. She'll be out of school soon."

"I'm only talking about a few weeks. Maybe she'd like to go to camp while we're away."

"She's only seven," Melissa protested.

"Almost eight, as she continually reminds you. There are camps geared for younger children. She'd love it."

"We'll see," Melissa answered evasively. "You have a trip to Wyoming coming up first. When are you leaving?"

"Tomorrow, I'm afraid. I'll miss you, sweetheart." He leaned forward and kissed her.

"Just remember you're a married man now, so no hanky-panky."

"What kind of trouble could I get into in the wilds of Wyoming?" He laughed.

Melissa missed Granger even more than she'd expected. They'd spent every moment together since their marriage, and now she was at loose ends. Betsy was in school most of the day, and everyone else she knew was working.

To escape from the silent house and Mrs. Flannery, Melissa swam and spent time in the garden. But swimming wasn't much fun alone, and the new gardener took excellent care of the grounds.

Melissa waited expectantly every night for Granger to call. He usually phoned about seven when they finished shooting. It was the high point of her day. He always told her how much he missed her, but the short conversations were unsatisfying. After she hung up, the long lonely evening stretched ahead and doubts plagued her. If Granger really wanted her with him, he would have asked her to come along. Was he secretly relieved to get away by himself?

Melissa told herself not to be so insecure, but in the middle of the week she began to wonder if her fears weren't valid. Granger called as usual, and they chatted about ordinary things. But this time Melissa could hear voices in the background.

"Is someone with you?" she asked.

"I'm using the phone in John's trailer—John Henning, the director," Granger explained. "We need to go over some changes in the script."

"It sounds as if you're working hard," Melissa commented.

"Everybody is. We're trying to get this wrapped up as fast as possible. Postproduction takes cost money."

Just then a woman called to him. "Granger, come over here when you get off the phone. We need you to settle a bet."

"Who was that?" Melissa asked sharply.

"Deborah Caldwell, my costar."

"I thought you said you'd be all alone out there."

Granger laughed. "You obviously *haven't* ever been on a movie set. There are always dozens of people around."

"You didn't mention any women."

"Don't tell me you're jealous?" His voice held an undercurrent of excitement.

Melissa was too intent on covering up her emotions to hear it. "Of course not, merely surprised. I've been feeling sorry for you for no reason," she said lightly.

"It's good of you to be concerned," he answered ironically.

"What do you want to drink, Granger?" a female voice in the background called, a different woman this time. "Kevin is bartending."

"There seems to be a party going on," Melissa remarked casually.

"The cast and crew are just unwinding a little before dinner. It was a long, dusty day."

"Don't disappear on me again tonight, Granger," a man's voice called. "We have to go over those changes."

"I'd better go, honey," Granger said to Melissa. "It's getting to be a madhouse around here. Do you want to tell me anything else?"

"No. Just . . . take care of yourself."

"You, too. I miss you, angel."

Melissa hung up slowly. When Granger said he was going to a distant outpost in the countryside, it hadn't occurred to her that he'd have a lot of company, both male and female.

If there were going to be that many people around, why did he assume she'd be bored? Of course they'd be working all day and she wouldn't, but was that really what concerned him?

Granger was the center of her universe, but she obviously wasn't essential to *him*. After two weeks of constant companionship, was he starting to feel smothered? Even if she was letting her imagination run riot, it was time to take a good long look at her life.

This was just a preview. Eventually Granger would go back to work, and the situation would repeat itself, only for months instead of a week. She had to develop her own interests. It wasn't healthy to be this dependent on one person.

What avenues were open to her, though? Even if she had any skills, it would hardly be feasible to take a job. Wouldn't the tabloids love *that?* Star's wife forced to work for a living. No, that solution was out, but what did other women in her position do?

Suddenly Melissa stopped pacing as an idea hit her. She could go to college and become a landscape architect as she'd originally planned. It would take years. First she'd have to get a degree, and then there would be graduate work, but no matter how long it took, she'd be working toward something worthwhile.

Granger would be so proud of her. Back when they hardly knew each other, he'd urged her to pursue her dream. Melissa was so excited that she almost phoned to tell him the news. Having second thoughts, she decided to keep it as a surprise. He was surrounded by people, and they wouldn't really be able to talk. This was too momentous a decision to skim over lightly. Tomorrow she'd drive to U.C.L.A. to fill out a registration form. By the time Granger returned, the dream would be a reality.

Melissa walked up the broad brick steps of the beautiful university, feeling both elated and self-conscious. All of the students swirling around her were young and casually dressed in jeans and T-shirts. They looked like the young carefree people in soft drink commercials. Would she ever fit in here?

Reminding herself that she wasn't coming for the social life, she read the names on the bewildering procession of brick buildings. Finally she located the admissions office. It was swarming with people, since summer classes were due to start shortly.

After taking an application form from a pile on a table, Melissa looked around for a place to fill it out. Everyone seemed to be using a book or a ring binder balanced on their knees. She found an empty chair in a row along one wall and tried to improvise, using her purse. It wasn't very successful.

"Are you having trouble?" a deep male voice asked.

"I'm afraid so," she answered. "My purse is too squashy to write on."

"You can borrow my notebook if you like."

She glanced up to thank him and received a surprise. The man was about thirty. He didn't look any more like a student than she did, although he was dressed like one in jeans, running shoes and a sweatshirt. The outfit didn't disguise his maturity. He looked like a surveyor, or maybe a forest ranger, something to do with the outdoors. His blond hair was bleached from the sun, and there were tiny lines around his blue eyes. He was a very attractive man.

Melissa suddenly realized she was staring. "Thanks very much," she said hastily, accepting the binder.

"Glad to be of help."

They both concentrated on filling out the lengthy forms for a while, but she came to a part that stumped her. After failing to figure it out, she said hesitantly, "Excuse me. Do you happen to know if line twelve applies to freshmen?"

"You're a first-year student?" He couldn't conceal his surprise.

"Hard to believe, isn't it?" she asked ruefully. "I already feel like a dinosaur."

He smiled, showing even white teeth. "From the pictures I've seen, they weren't nearly as attractive."

She returned his smile. "How did you know I needed a kind word?"

"College seems a bit intimidating at first, even to an adult. Don't be discouraged. You'll get the hang of it."

"I hope so. What year are you in?"

"I'm in graduate school. I'm going for a degree in architecture."

"What a coincidence!" Melissa exclaimed. "That's the field I'm interested in. I hope to be a landscape architect some day."

"We seem to have a lot in common." He held out his hand. "I'm Sean Crosley."

"Melissa Fairfield," she said without thinking, then neglected to correct the error. It was just as well to keep a low profile. "What branch of architecture are you interested in?" she asked.

They were deep in conversation when a woman came out of an office and announced, "Anyone waiting to speak to a counselor, come to window four."

When Sean stood up, Melissa held out his notebook. "Thanks for the loan."

"You aren't through yet. Keep it until you're finished."

"You might be in the counselor's office by then," she said.

"It won't take me long. I just have one or two questions. If you're not in a hurry, perhaps you can wait for me. I could give you some pointers over a cup of coffee."

"I'd really appreciate any advice."

She watched him walk away, admiring his tall, broad-shouldered physique in a purely clinical sense. Sean was an interesting man. She wondered what his story was, why he'd delayed his education.

He told her while they were having coffee on a bench in the plaza. It was such a lovely day that they'd patronized one of the many stands scattered throughout the campus instead of going to the student union.

"I just love it here, even if I do feel out of place with all these young kids," Melissa commented, glancing around.

"A lot of people put their schooling on hold for one reason or another," Sean said. "Look at me. I knocked around the world for a few years after I got my B.A."

"That sounds romantic."

"It wasn't exactly a picnic. I worked on a freighter doing manual labor, but I did get to see some spectacular places."

"Why did you give it up?"

"When I hit thirty I decided it was time to settle down and start thinking about the future. How about you?" he asked. "Why did you postpone going to college?"

"The usual story. I got married and had a child right away."

"At least you had a good reason." He glanced at her diamond wedding band. "A happy marriage is quite an accomplishment these days."

She didn't enlighten him any further. "With all the traveling you did, I don't suppose you had time to get married."

He looked out over the campus. "I was engaged in college. She was killed in an automobile accident right after we graduated. That was the reason I dropped out."

"I'm so sorry," Melissa apologized. "I shouldn't have asked."

"It's all right. It was a long time ago, and I've learned to live with it." He changed the subject. "What does your husband think about you going back to school?"

"I haven't told him yet. He's out of town. I plan to surprise him with the news."

Sean smiled. "I hope for your sake he likes surprises."

"Granger is the dearest man in the whole world. He'll be happy for me. He knows I've always felt I missed out on a lot."

"If I can help you find your way around, just say the word."

"Thanks, but unfortunately I won't be starting classes until September. I found out I can't get into the summer session."

"Time passes quickly," he consoled her.

"I know, but I'm so anxious to get started. Can I ask you some questions about beginning courses?"

Melissa eagerly drank in all the information he gave her. She wasn't aware of the time until he glanced at his watch. "I'm sorry. I'm keeping you from something," she said.

"I do have an appointment," he admitted.

"Well, it's been great talking to you. I really appreciate the orientation course."

"I'll give you my phone number in case you have any questions." He tore a sheet of paper out of his notebook and scribbled on it. "I'll also try to find out those grade requirements you asked about."

"That would be very helpful." After a moment's hesitation, Melissa gave him her own phone number. Sean hadn't made the slightest attempt to hit on her, and he knew she was married, so why not? She was lucky to have a friend in this huge sprawling place.

* * *

Melissa could hardly wait for Granger to come home that Friday. He'd promised to be home for dinner, and Mrs. Flannery was cooking up a storm. All had not gone smoothly that day, however. Betsy and the housekeeper had had another run-in.

The continuing friction between the two was discouraging. There was no way Melissa could go away and leave them alone just yet. Granger's plans for a honeymoon would simply have to be put on hold—for who knew how long?

"Mac's here! He's home!" Betsy called excitedly, late in the afternoon.

Melissa's anticipation was even greater than Betsy's as she went to the front door to greet him. She took a quick peek in the hall mirror, hoping she looked as glamorous in her blue silk caftan as the woman he'd been on location with.

Granger's greeting allayed all her fears. After one burning glance, he took her in his arms and held her so tightly that she could hardly breathe.

"God, how I've missed you!" he muttered, burying his face in her neck.

"I'm glad you're home," she said, in a massive understatement.

Their reunion was brief. Betsy and Clancy were also overjoyed to see Granger. The dog barked and raced around him in circles, and the little girl tugged at his arm for attention.

"Guess what? I taught Clancy a new trick. Isn't that neat?"

"Astounding." Granger chuckled. "I didn't think he did *anything* he was told to."

"Do you want to see it?" she asked.

"In a few minutes. First I want to talk to your mom and find out what's been happening while I was away."

"She's going to go to school," Betsy announced.

Granger looked at Melissa in surprise. "You plan to take a course in something?"

"No, she's going to school every day, just like me," Betsy said.

This wasn't the way Melissa wanted to break the news. "Give Mac a chance to relax and take off his jacket. Would you like a drink, darling?" she asked him.

"That would be nice." He looked at her speculatively as they walked toward the den. "What's all this about school?"

"We'll talk about it later when we're alone," she promised.

A smile tilted his lips as he hooked one hand around the nape of her neck and gazed into her eyes. "I hope it's a short subject."

Chapter Ten

Melissa and Granger didn't get around to talking until much later that night. As soon as the door of their bedroom closed, he took her in his arms and kissed her passionately.

"I thought we'd never be alone," he groaned.

She laughed breathlessly. "That's what happens when you're a family man. You can't make love whenever you get the urge."

"That happens every time I'm near you." He slipped the caftan off her shoulder and strung a line of kisses over her bare skin. "Have I told you how beautiful you are?"

"Not for a week," she murmured.

"Is that all it was? It felt like an eternity." He cupped her bottom in both hands and guided her hips against his. "I don't ever want to be away from you again."

He kissed her ardently, probing the warm recess of her mouth until Melissa turned liquid with desire. She unbuttoned his shirt and slid her hands inside, gliding her palms over his flat nipples.

"Ahh, darling, I love it when you touch me," he said huskily.

"I love it, too," she whispered.

Her hands moved to his belt buckle, and then to the zipper of his slacks. As they slid down, she urged his shorts over his hips and caressed him intimately.

Granger stood rigidly for a few moments, allowing her to fondle him. Then he gave a hoarse cry. "You're too much for any man to resist."

He kicked aside his clothes and removed hers with the same frantic haste. Their bodies met and moved against each other tantalizingly. It was sweet torture, a preliminary taste of the rapture that lay in store.

When Granger reached the limit of endurance, he carried Melissa to the bed and buried himself inside of her. They became one person, experiencing the same molten spirals of sensation, the same cresting burst of wonder, and finally the same release from tension.

Afterward he stroked her gently. "This is what I missed. I don't like sleeping alone."

"Is that the only reason you missed me?"

"It's a pretty good one." He chuckled.

"I guess so," she answered dully. Granger still hadn't said he loved her, not even during the heat of passion.

"Is something wrong, sweetheart?" He was instantly attuned to her mood.

She gazed at his handsome face in the moonlight and felt her heart lurch. At least she had this. Granger had fulfilled his part of the bargain. She shouldn't complain.

"What could be wrong?" she asked softly.

He propped his head on one hand. "Tell me about this school thing. What's going on?"

Melissa's faint melancholy disappeared. She sat up against the headboard, her face animated. "I'm really excited about it." She told him what she'd done in his absence.

Granger's reaction wasn't what she expected. "You signed up for a full schedule?" he asked, frowning. "That means you'll have classes every day."

"I'm really serious about this, Granger. I want to get my degree and then go on to grad school."

"I understand, but couldn't you take a few courses at a time?"

"It will take me four years just to get my B.A.," she explained patiently. "If I only go part-time, I'll never get through."

"What's the big rush?"

"I don't want to be the oldest living landscape architect in L.A.," she answered, a trifle tartly.

"Has it occurred to you that we won't have any time together?" he asked evenly.

"We'll have evenings and weekends."

"We share those with other people. I thought you enjoyed the days we spent alone together, doing whatever we felt like."

"I did! But that can't last forever. You'll go back to work sooner or later. Your desk is piled high with new scripts that your agent sent over."

"I don't have to accept them. I like the life we were leading."

"Be reasonable, Granger. Eventually you'll find a script that appeals to you, and then *you'll* be gone all day. I can't exist in a vacuum, just waiting for you to come home.'' She looked at him appealingly. "I have to make a life for myself."

"I didn't realize you were unhappy," he said slowly.

"I'm not! These past weeks have been wonderful."

"Then why do you want to change things?"

"Try to understand," she pleaded. "Everyone has a dream. But if you don't pursue it, it will never come true. You were the one who told me that."

Granger's grim expression softened and he took her in his arms. "I'm sorry, angel. I'm being selfish. My only excuse is that I don't want to share you with anyone."

"You won't have to. The other students are young enough to be my kid brothers and sisters." Melissa didn't think it was prudent to mention Sean at this point. "All I'm going to share with them are classes."

"If this is what you want to do, then of course you should go for it," he said fondly.

"We'll still have a lot of time together."

"Sure, we can share milk and cookies after school," Granger answered dryly.

"Right, and you can help me with my homework." She smiled.

"That's the part I'm looking forward to." He wrapped his legs around hers and trailed his fingers down her spine. "I was always good at homework."

"I'd give you an A-plus," she murmured as their lips met.

Melissa was careful not to mention anything to do with college in the days that followed. She and Granger resumed their carefree existence, doing whatever appealed to them at the moment and making love spontaneously. Both were completely happy in each other's company.

They hadn't exchanged a sharp word since their marriage. A telephone call provoked their first quarrel.

They had come home from lunch at the Beverly Hills Hotel and decided to spend the rest of the afternoon by the pool. Granger was expecting a business call, so he'd brought the cordless phone outside. When it rang he climbed out of the water to answer it while Melissa continued to swim laps.

The caller had a deep male voice. "May I speak to Melissa Fairfield?" he asked.

Granger frowned. "Who is this?"

"Tell her it's Sean Crosley."

"What is this about? Does she know you?"

"We met in the admissions office at U.C.L.A. a few days ago. Are you her—?"

But Granger hadn't waited to hear any more. He put the phone down and called to Melissa, "It's for you."

She got out of the pool and grabbed a towel to dry her hands and face. "Who is it?"

"That's what I'd like to know," Granger answered evenly.

She raised her eyebrows as she reached for the phone. "Hello. This is Melissa."

"Hi, it's Sean Crosley. We met at U.C.L.A., remember?"

"Of course, but I didn't expect to hear from you." Melissa regretted giving him her phone number. She was very conscious of Granger standing nearby, listening openly.

"I thought you might be interested in a symposium on career choices being held at Ackerman Hall on Thursday night. George Clement Williamson is going to be one of the speakers. You know who he is, don't you?"

"Of course! He's the prize-winning landscape architect. I'd love to hear him speak."

"This is your chance," Sean told her. "The lecture starts at seven."

"Are you going?"

"I plan to. Do you want me to save you a seat?"

Melissa was abruptly aware of Granger. His expression had darkened alarmingly. "No, I...uh...I'll look for you if I can make it," she told Sean.

"Okay, I just wanted to let you know."

"That was very thoughtful of you. Thanks, Sean." Melissa hung up with a feeling of foreboding that was soon justified.

"Who was that?" Granger asked ominously.

"Just someone I met when I was registering," she replied dismissively.

"He didn't sound like the kid-brother type."

"Sean is a graduate student."

"That would make him what...twenty-two? Twenty-three?"

"More like thirty," she answered reluctantly.

"I see. I suppose that explains why you gave him your maiden name."

"That simply slipped out. I still have trouble believing I'm actually Mrs. McMasters." She smiled nervously. "When we were introducing ourselves, I just automatically said Melissa Fairfield."

"You didn't think it was worthwhile to correct the oversight?"

"I thought it was better not to. I'd rather nobody finds out I'm your wife." As Granger's face hardened into granite, she rushed on. "If the news gets out I'll be a curiosity—the woman who's married to Granger Mc-

Masters. Even the professors might treat me differently. I want to stand or fall on my own merits."

"I'm sorry I'm such a liability to you," he answered icily.

"You're deliberately misunderstanding. You, of all people know what it's like to be the center of attention. If that ever happens to me, at least I want to have done something to earn it."

"You didn't seem to mind *Sean's* attention. The two of you must have gotten very friendly if you gave him your phone number. Just how long did you spend with him?"

"I don't believe this!" she exclaimed. "Are you accusing me of being involved with a man I only met casually?"

"I'm not accusing you of anything. But you can hardly blame me for being unhappy over the fact that you didn't mention being married."

"I *did* mention it. The only reason Sean called was to tell me about a lecture on architecture."

"That he just happens to be attending, also."

"He's studying to be an architect!" she exclaimed in frustration. "He knew I'd be interested."

Granger's jaw became even more rigid. "You'll be taking classes together?"

"No, of course not. I told you, Sean is in grad school. I don't understand why you're making such a big deal out of this. Married people do have friends of the opposite sex. I don't object to *yours.*"

"When was the last time I had a date with a woman?" Granger demanded.

"I didn't have a date, but *you* spent last week *surrounded* by women!"

"They were members of the cast and crew, for Pete's sake. I was working!"

"That's not what it sounded like when you called me."
Melissa was as angry as Granger when she remembered
his phone call. "There seemed to be quite a party going
on."

"We were simply unwinding. I explained about that."

"And I accepted your explanation. Unlike you,"
Melissa added witheringly.

Granger's wrath subsided as he looked at her searchingly. "But you didn't really believe me?"

"Let's just say I'm more understanding than you are."

His austerity returned. "In the future I'll try to match
your indifference." He strode away before she could answer.

Melissa stared after him, completely baffled. What was
really behind Granger's tirade? He couldn't honestly
think she was having an affair, so why was he so upset
over her friendship with Sean? In a normal marriage,
jealousy would be the logical answer, but Granger wasn't
in love with her. His behavior just now was merely chau-
vinistic, she decided: husbands can fool around, but
wives can't. He'd certainly ended the conversation swiftly
when she'd brought up those parties on location, Melissa reflected bitterly.

Granger stayed in his office for the rest of the afternoon. He didn't come out until dinnertime.

Betsy immediately monopolized his attention, so dinner wasn't the awkward situation it might have been—
because Granger hadn't gotten over his pique. He was his
old self with Betsy, however. They laughed and joked
together while Melissa picked at her food.

After Betsy had gone to bed there was no longer a
buffer between Granger and Melissa. She ached to break
through his cool courtesy, but she didn't know how. He
read a book in silence, and she watched television. They

were together in the same room, but they might as well have been at opposite poles.

Melissa began to feel resentful. If Granger wanted to act childishly, let him! Her conscience was clear.

When the eleven-o'clock news was over she clicked off the TV set. "I'm tired," she remarked, yawning elaborately. "I'm going to bed."

"Good night," he answered without glancing up.

Melissa's annoyance was replaced by desolation as she undressed and got into bed. Granger didn't want to make up. That showed how much she meant to him.

She wasn't the slightest bit tired, but after claiming to be, she had to turn out the light. Sleep was still eluding her when Granger came to bed about an hour later.

He got undressed by the light coming through the windows, quietly so as not to disturb her, which deepened Melissa's misery. She couldn't help watching him, though, as he padded around the room removing his clothes. When he glanced over at the bed she quickly closed her eyes, but a picture of his splendid nude body remained printed on her eyelids.

She simulated even breathing when Granger got into bed, although it wasn't necessary. He turned on his side—the one away from her.

It took a long time, but eventually Melissa fell asleep. She awakened sometime in the middle of the night, uncertain of what had disturbed her. It soon became apparent. Granger had wrapped a lock of her hair around his forefinger. His head was propped on one hand and he was gazing at her with an expression she couldn't fathom. It almost looked like sadness.

When her eyes opened he said, "I'm sorry. I didn't mean to wake you."

"Is anything wrong?" she asked uncertainly.

He sighed. "You know there is. I behaved like a jerk."

"I guess we both overreacted a little this afternoon."

"No. You were honest with me and I couldn't take it."

She sat up and stared at him in bewilderment. "I've *always* been honest with you."

"I know. We both went into this marriage for our own reasons. But I'd hoped—" He broke off to choose his words more carefully. "I suppose my ego was hurt that you thought I was fooling around and it didn't bother you."

"I never said that!"

"You didn't have to. A normal wife would have thrown a tantrum."

The way he did? Melissa's heart almost stopped at the implication. Did Granger really care about her deeply? She had to find out without forcing him to say something he didn't mean just to smooth over their differences.

"Ours isn't a conventional marriage," she began hesitantly. "I don't feel I can make any demands on you."

"Not even for fidelity?"

"I didn't suspect you of being unfaithful. I know how women flock around you, but I also know you're not promiscuous. I guess I was aggravated that you could enjoy yourself without me, but I wasn't allowed the same privilege."

"That's perfectly valid except that I was thrown together with those people. I didn't seek them out."

"It was the same with me. Sean and I met accidentally. We struck up a friendship because we have common interests."

"That don't include me," Granger said quietly. "I guess that's really what this is all about. I fulfilled my function in your life, and now you don't need me anymore."

"That's not so! I don't know what I'd do without you."

"You're on your way to finding out." He smoothed her hair gently. "I showed you there's a whole world out there. Sooner or later you'll meet someone you want to spend the rest of your life with."

How could she tell him she already had, when he was giving her his blessing, albeit reluctantly. Melissa swallowed hard and said, "The same holds true for you."

"I'm satisfied with our arrangement." His eyes were unreadable in the dim light.

"I am, too," she answered hopelessly. She'd given him every opportunity, but Granger still hadn't said he loved her, merely that he was satisfied.

"Then I guess that means our marriage is still working." He gave her a lopsided smile. "Are we friends again?"

She mustered a tiny smile of her own. "I hope we always will be. It would be a shame to let marriage break up a beautiful friendship."

"At least we'll always have that." Granger's voice held a trace of irony. "Good night, angel."

He leaned over to kiss her. It was meant to be a casual good-night kiss, but no physical contact between was ever casual. Melissa's lips parted and she put her arm around his waist.

Granger reacted immediately, drawing her into a close embrace. "This is what I wanted to do all evening," he muttered, gliding his hands over her body.

"You didn't come near me," she said reproachfully. "You even let me go to bed alone."

"I thought you didn't want me. You don't know what torture that was."

"There's never been a time when I didn't want you," she murmured, sliding her palms inside the drawstring of his pajama bottoms.

Melissa didn't care if she was revealing too much. The joy of having Granger back was all that mattered. She caressed his hardened body until he was rigid with the effort at self-control.

Finally he stripped off her gown, tearing it in his frenzied haste. When they were both nude, he clasped her tightly, making her aware of his throbbing desire.

"What would I do without you?" he groaned.

"You won't ever have to find out." She dug her fingers into his buttocks, urging their hips even closer. "This is what you want, isn't it?"

"Yes, oh yes," she breathed.

He lifted his head to gaze at her passion-filled face. "Is that all? Only this?"

She moved against him restlessly. "No, I want all of you."

He continued to stare at her for a moment, until her sensuous movements drove everything else from his mind.

Granger was inspired that night. They were both frantic, as much with the desire to give pleasure as to receive it. Their actions were a substitute for deeply buried feelings.

Afterward, as Melissa lay spent in Granger's arms, he sighed and murmured almost inaudibly, "It will have to be enough."

She wanted to question him, but in her languid state, it was too much of an effort. Many of the things Granger had said were puzzling. Melissa wanted to figure them out, but she couldn't concentrate. Her breathing slowed and she drifted off to sleep.

After that, Granger and Melissa were elaborately careful about what they said to each other. Neither wanted to risk another argument. But gradually they resumed their former unself-conscious relationship.

"At least our quarrel had one good result," Granger joked when they were back on their old footing. "I found a script I like."

"Don't tell me you're going back to work? I thought you intended to loaf for the rest of your life," she teased.

"I figured I'd better get out from underfoot before you and Mrs. Flannery walked out in protest."

"She wouldn't leave you if you were radioactive," Melissa answered a trifle grimly.

Her tone wasn't lost on him. "Is there a problem? I thought Mrs. Flannery and Betsy were getting along fine."

"Little things come up in the best of families. It's no big deal."

Melissa didn't want to tell him that the difficulty was far from resolved. Just the day before, Betsy and the housekeeper had engaged in another skirmish. Melissa was losing faith in an ultimate truce, but she kept doggedly trying to keep the peace. Granger was the only one who thought she'd succeeded.

When his deal was signed and he went to work, Melissa asked again to visit the set.

"As soon as we start shooting," he promised. "Right now we're only having meetings and doing readthroughs. It isn't very interesting."

"You keep saying that. I'll bet you're actually rehearsing torrid love scenes, and you don't want me to watch," Melissa teased.

"That's a safe bet." He pulled her onto his lap and nibbled on her ear. "How could I concentrate on another woman if you were anywhere in the vicinity?"

She mussed his hair playfully. "What movie was *that* line from?"

He gazed at her enigmatically. "You're a tough lady to convince."

"Maybe I'm just afraid to believe in my own good fortune," she answered lightly.

Granger hesitated. "Melissa, I think it's time we—" He didn't get to finish.

Betsy came racing into the room. "Mac! Mac! You have to come quick! A cat got in the yard, and Clancy is chasing it."

A few days after that, Granger came home in high spirits. "All the preproduction work is finished and we're ready to start shooting," he announced.

"Does that mean I can finally visit you on the set?" Melissa asked.

"Every day if you like. We're shooting the first scenes in London."

"You didn't tell me the picture was being made in Europe!" Her spirits sank. That meant he could be gone for months.

"Only part of it. I play a businessman who goes to London for a vacation and gets mixed up in a spy ring. It's all very complicated. I'll give you the script to read."

Melissa was more interested in fact than fiction. "How long will you be over there?"

"We're budgeted for six weeks, but there are usually delays. It will probably be more like two months."

"Well, that's very exciting news." She tried to sound enthusiastic.

"I thought you'd be pleased. We leave day after tomorrow. I'm sorry I couldn't give you more notice, angel, but it's typical of the industry."

"That's all right. The sooner you leave, the sooner you'll be home," she said brightly.

He looked surprised. "What do you mean? You're coming with me."

"I couldn't possibly!" she gasped.

He frowned. "Of course you can. What's stopping you?"

"Betsy for one thing. I couldn't leave her for two months."

"I hadn't thought of that," Granger said reluctantly. "Oh well, we'll play it by ear. You can come with me for a couple of weeks, and maybe when Betsy gets out of school she can join us." His enthusiasm returned. "I'll take you to Paris one weekend. There's so much I want to show you."

"I can't even go for two weeks," Melissa said quietly.

His animation died. "You mean you don't want to."

"There's nothing I'd love more, but I can't leave Betsy alone with Mrs. Flannery."

"You told me everything was straightened out."

"I didn't want to bother you with my problems. I really thought Mrs. Flannery would accept us once we were living here, but I'm beginning to think it's hopeless. She bitterly resents me, and she detests Betsy. They're at swords' points every day."

"Why didn't you tell me this before?" Granger asked explosively.

"I didn't want you to fire her. Mrs. Flannery has devoted her life to you."

"I realize that, and I'm sorry it's come to this. But if the situation is as bad as you say, she must be unhappy, too. It will be a wrench at first, but she'll be better off in the long run. Mrs. Flannery clearly has to go."

"I'm afraid you're right, but let me do it. I'd rather she'd be angry than hurt."

Granger cupped Melissa's cheek in his palm. "Have I ever told you that you're a very nice person?"

"Look where it got me." She smiled ruefully. "I've always wanted to go to Europe."

"You can still come. Hire a new housekeeper and join me next week. That might be even better," he mused. "We'll be organized by then and I'll have more time to spend with you."

"I couldn't leave Betsy with a stranger."

"We've been through this before, Melissa." Granger's eyes took on a steely glint. "Go to a reputable agency and check the woman's credentials thoroughly. I'm not asking you to hire her one day and leave the next. You'll know in a week if she's reliable."

"That isn't long enough to really know someone, and besides, I can't just boot Mrs. Flannery out without notice."

"I wouldn't want you to. Give her three months salary and tell her she can stay until she finds another position. I don't want to be unfeeling."

"It isn't that simple." Melissa remembered the older woman's panic, her pitiful admission that she wouldn't know where to go.

"It's exactly that simple." Granger's jaw set grimly. "If you really wanted to be with me, you'd find a way."

Melissa looked at him steadily. "It isn't fair to ask me to choose between you and Betsy. She's only a child. She needs me."

"And I don't?" he demanded.

"Not in the same way."

"Of course not! You're my wife. But I'm concerned about Betsy, too. She's very dear to me. Do you honestly think I'd ask you to neglect her?"

"No, but you're not a mother. You don't understand."

A muscle bunched at the point of his jaw. "I've tried to be a father to her, but evidently I've failed in your eyes."

"I never said that! You've been wonderful with Betsy. She adores you."

"It's nice to know I've lived up to *somebody's* expectations."

"Please don't do this to me, Granger. I feel as if I'm being torn in two."

His iciness melted when he saw the tears lurking in her eyes. "I'm sorry, darling. I guess I can't expect you to change overnight. You've had sole responsibility for Betsy for seven years. I just wish you could believe that I care about her, too."

"I know you do. Maybe I *am* overly cautious. I don't mean to be, but she's so vulnerable."

"We all are, sweetheart, but you can't stop living because you might get hurt." Granger's face held sadness. "You have to believe everything will work out."

"You're right, of course. I'll try to lighten up. If I can find an adequate housekeeper, I'll join you in London later on."

He wasn't convinced by Melissa's vague promise, but he recognized the futility of arguing the matter further.

"At least start by giving Mrs. Flannery notice. That situation has gone on too long."

"I'll do it after you leave," she promised.

Melissa fully intended to keep her word, but she didn't want to fire the woman on the day after Granger left. That would look too calculated. She decided to wait until the next flare-up between Betsy and Mrs. Flannery, a predictable occurrence. Then, at least, the housekeeper would realize she had to share the blame.

It wasn't long after Granger left, however, that Melissa had more to worry about than her petty problems at home. Stories about Granger began appearing in the tabloids almost immediately, linking him romantically with his current costar.

Crystal Parsons was a stunningly beautiful redhead who had been publicly involved with several of the male stars she'd worked with. She was glamorous, uninhibited and outspoken—a natural target for the tabloids. She and Granger together were a bonanza!

Stories about them hinted at a flaming romance, while speculating on whether Granger's marriage was already on the skids. Melissa hung up on more than one reporter who attempted to interview her.

She tried to tell herself that such trash was beneath contempt. Granger had told her they never bothered with the truth because a lie sold more papers. But when he phoned that afternoon, she couldn't keep the coolness out of her voice.

Granger, on the other hand, was in high spirits. "Everything's going great, angel. It feels good to be back in harness again. We have a fine crew, and even the weather is terrific."

"I'm glad you're having a good time," she remarked tepidly.

"Well, I wouldn't say that. I'm over here to work—although we did see an excellent play last night."

"We, meaning you and Crystal?"

"No, I went with Larry Weston, the director."

"That's a surprise. The *National Informer* says you and Crystal seldom leave each other's side."

Granger made a sound of disgust. "So what else is new? You know better than to believe the garbage they print."

"Crystal has quite a reputation," Melissa maintained stubbornly. "She had affairs with three of her previous costars. Perhaps she wants to add you to the list."

"That's sheer nonsense. Only one of those stories about her had a grain of truth. She's a really nice kid. You'd like her."

"If you say so," Melissa answered neutrally.

"You don't honestly believe there's something going on between us?" Granger exclaimed.

"Maybe not, but it doesn't delight me to read that our marriage is on the rocks." Her pent-up resentment burst forth.

"If you were here with me, there wouldn't be any basis for gossip," he replied evenly.

"What am I supposed to do, trail around after you like a guard dog? That's demeaning!"

"Then I guess you'll just have to live with the consequences. You should have known what it would be like when you married me."

"I don't have to enjoy it," she muttered.

The hard note in Granger's voice softened. "I know it's annoying, honey, but you have to keep your perspective. The best thing to do is not even read that trash."

"You're probably right." She sighed.

"I know I am. Don't give it another thought. I have to study my lines now, but I'll call you tomorrow."

Melissa hung up slowly, not at all reassured. Granger hadn't asked if she'd interviewed housekeepers or when she might be able to join him in London.

Were those articles making her overreact? Melissa couldn't really believe he was having an affair with his costar. Crystal was a gorgeous woman, though, and he was feeling unappreciated at home. That was a potentially explosive situation.

Melissa told herself it was beneath her dignity to compete for her own husband, but that didn't make her feel any better. There was one thing she could do, however. The problem of Mrs. Flannery wouldn't go away by itself. Right now was a good time to settle it, since her spirits couldn't get much lower.

Mrs. Flannery was in the kitchen chopping cabbage with a wickedly sharp knife. She seemed to be enjoying every slashing stroke, as though they relieved her frustrations.

Melissa led up to the unpleasant task ahead with a little preliminary small talk. "Is that coleslaw you're making?" she asked.

"Do you want something else for a salad? You didn't tell me that," the housekeeper said sullenly.

Melissa stifled a sigh. If she'd had any doubts, they vanished. Mrs. Flannery had to go. "Coleslaw will be fine." She hesitated for a moment. "Wouldn't it be easier to use the food processor?"

"I have my own way of doing things."

"That's what I want to talk to you about," Melissa began.

The flashing knife paused for a moment as the woman looked at her suspiciously. "What has that child been telling you about me now?"

"Betsy didn't say anything. This is something you and I have to settle."

"She's always trying to get me in trouble," the housekeeper muttered.

At that moment Betsy came into the kitchen, and Mrs. Flannery resumed her chopping, even more furiously.

"Can I have something to eat?" Betsy opened the door of the refrigerator. "Oh goody, chocolate pudding."

"It isn't ready yet," the housekeeper said without looking up. "It's still warm."

"I like it warm." Betsy reached into the refrigerator and took out a large bowl of pudding with one hand and a half gallon of milk with the other.

"Don't try to carry both of them at once," Melissa called.

Her warning came too late. The heavy carton slipped out of the little girl's hand and milk spilled on the floor. As Mrs. Flannery glanced up with a scowl, the knife slipped and blood spurted out of a deep gash in her hand.

When she simply stared at it mutely, Melissa grabbed a length of paper towels to staunch the flow. "Get the first-aid kit out of Mac's bathroom," she instructed Betsy.

But by the time the child returned, Melissa realized that Mrs. Flannery needed more than first aid. She quickly swaddled the injured hand in a clean dish towel and helped the older woman to her feet. Mrs. Flannery seemed dazed.

"Is she going to die?" Betsy's eyes were wide with apprehension as she stared at the blood seeping through the white towel.

"Of course not! She's going to be fine. We'll just go to the emergency hospital, because they can bandage her hand better than I can."

Melissa's bright tone covered hidden panic. The woman was in shock and losing a lot of blood. If only Granger were here! For the first time she understood what he was trying to tell her about sharing.

Chapter Eleven

A nurse rushed Mrs. Flannery into an inner room of the emergency hospital, telling Melissa and Betsy to wait outside. The little girl was very chastened.

"It was my fault, wasn't it?" she asked in a tiny voice.

"Not really. It was an accident," Melissa answered.

"I don't like Mrs. Flannery very much, but I didn't want her to get hurt."

"I know you didn't, honey," Melissa said gently.

"I'll try not to make her mad at me from now on," Betsy promised solemnly. "Are you sure she'll be all right?"

"Yes, I'm sure of it," Melissa answered, trying to sound confident.

She was abruptly aware of the consequences of this accident. What if Mrs. Flannery had severed a major artery? The amount of blood that gushed out had been frightening. Even if her hand wasn't permanently damaged, she wouldn't be able to use it for some time. Under the circumstances, Melissa couldn't possibly ask her to leave. The woman had no place to go and no one to take care of her.

The doctor appeared a short time later. "She'll be out in a few minutes. The nurse is bandaging the hand now." He handed Melissa a small white envelope. "These pills are for pain. I had to take stitches, so she might have some discomfort. I'd advise you to keep her in bed today. This had been a shock to her nervous system."

"Will she regain full use of that hand?" Melissa asked anxiously.

"I don't foresee any problems. No ligaments were cut, fortunately. You might want to take her to your own physician in a day or two, to be sure the wound is healing properly."

"I'll do that. Thank you, Doctor."

Mrs. Flannery's face was drawn when she came out of the emergency room. She was silent on the drive home, but it wasn't a sullen silence. She still seemed slightly dazed. Clearly the shock hadn't worn off.

Betsy was also subdued. When they reached the house she went around to the backyard while Melissa helped Mrs. Flannery to her room.

"Just sit in this chair for a minute until I fix your bed, and then I'll help you get undressed," Melissa told her.

"I have to start dinner," the housekeeper said vaguely.

"I'll do that. You're going to stay in bed and rest."

Melissa removed the spread and turned down the covers. Then she helped the older woman out of her clothes and into a plain white cotton nightgown.

"Try to take a little nap now. I'll look in on you later." She pulled down the blinds before going out and closing the bedroom door.

Melissa felt like a stranger in her own kitchen. She didn't know where anything was kept or what Mrs. Flannery had planned for dinner. A search of the refrigerator yielded a chicken and some fresh broccoli. She decided on mashed potatoes and a tossed green salad to round out the meal, with cookies and ice cream for dessert.

The unaccustomed activity took Melissa's mind off her troubles, and she felt herself relaxing. When the chicken was turning a golden brown under the broiler, she called to Betsy from the breakfast room window.

"Come in and wash your hands, honey. After I fix a tray for Mrs. Flannery, we'll have dinner."

Melissa had found a white wicker breakfast-tray stand on a top shelf in one of the kitchen cabinets. She took it to the housekeeper's room, tapped on the door and went in. The older woman was lying quietly in bed, but her eyes were open.

"Do you feel better after your rest?" Melissa asked. "The doctor sent along some pills in case you're in pain. I put them on your nightstand next to the glass of water."

"I don't need anything. My hand just throbs a little," Mrs. Flannery said, watching Melissa pull up the shades.

"It's foolish to suffer if you don't have to. Be sure to take one if you need it." Melissa placed the wicker stand over the housekeeper's knees. "I'll be back in a minute with your dinner."

She returned with a laden tray, to which she'd added a crystal bell. "If you want anything else, just ring the bell. I'll come back in a little while with your dessert. We're having ice cream, and I didn't want it to melt while you're eating your dinner."

The older woman seemed agitated, but before she could say anything, Betsy came into the room. She was carrying a large bunch of flowers she'd picked in the garden.

The little girl's face was apprehensive, but she hesitantly approached the bed and held out the bouquet. "I'm sorry you got hurt," she murmured.

Mrs. Flannery's reaction was totally unexpected. She burst into tears and covered her face with her good hand.

Betsy turned to Melissa, her soft mouth trembling. "I thought she'd like them."

"Mrs. Flannery is just a little upset, darling," Melissa said soothingly. "It was a lovely thing to do. Take the flowers into the kitchen and put them in water." When the child had left the room Melissa said, "She really meant well. Betsy feels bad about your accident."

"I thought she hated me. I thought you both did." The housekeeper sobbed louder.

Melissa patted her shoulder gingerly. "We've all had our differences, but we certainly don't hate you."

"You have every reason to. I've made your life miserable from the very beginning. I said horrid things and I wouldn't let you enjoy your own home. I've given you nothing but trouble." The self-recriminations came tumbling out one after another.

Melissa couldn't pretend the accusations weren't true, but she tried to minimize them. "I know how you feel about Mr. McMasters. I'm just sorry you couldn't see that I wasn't a threat."

Mrs. Flannery stared at her helplessly. "After all I've done to you, how could you be so good to me?"

Melissa looked surprised. "What did I do?"

"You rushed me to the hospital. You cooked dinner and even brought it to me here in bed."

"That's just simple humanity. I'm sure you'd do the same for me."

"I don't know what to say." The woman's tears started again. "Can you ever forgive me?"

"I have a better idea. Why don't we forget all the unpleasantness and simply start over?"

"Mr. McMasters is lucky to have found someone like you," Mrs. Flannery said in a choked voice.

Melissa realized she's been given the highest accolade. She kept her voice light to hide the lump in her throat. "I guess you could say he's blessed with three fantastic females."

"Would you ask Betsy to come back so I can thank her for the flowers?" Mrs. Flannery asked humbly.

After that fateful day everything changed dramatically. Mrs. Flannery was like a different person. All the love she'd lavished on Granger now expanded to include Melissa and Betsy. She couldn't do enough for them, even with only one good hand. But it wasn't only that. Little by little the older woman learned to smile, and even to make small jokes. It was like seeing an ugly caterpiller turn into a butterfly.

Melissa regretted the accident, but she certainly welcomed the result. Everything was turning out as she'd hoped. At least on the home front. Granger was another matter.

He continued to telephone regularly, but Melissa sensed a certain coolness in his manner. Was she imagining it? If so, why didn't he ever ask when she'd be joining him?

Melissa didn't tell him about Mrs. Flannery's metamorphosis. It was a long story, and she still couldn't leave Betsy until the housekeeper's hand healed. They continued to exchange bits of news like two casual friends, except at the end of the conversation. Granger always dutifully told her he missed her, and she expressed the same sentiment, keeping her voice as detached as his.

Melissa's unhappiness grew with every new article about Granger and Crystal—and there were many. She didn't mention them to him again, however, knowing he'd give the same answer. It was all baseless gossip.

She tried to take Granger's advice and avoid the tabloids, but even the entertainment section of the daily newspapers carried articles about their activities in London. Granger and Crystal were big stars. Melissa's spirits were at low ebb when Sean Crosley telephoned.

"I wasn't sure if it was all right to call you again," he began cautiously.

"Why would you think that?" she asked. "I'm delighted to hear from you."

"Your husband didn't seem too pleased the last time I phoned, and you didn't come to the lecture."

"Granger was a little...uh... preoccupied when he talked to you. I'm really sorry I missed the lecture. I'd forgotten about a previous engagement."

"I took a chance that it was something like that. The reason I called is to tell you that Williamson is speaking to our architecture class on Tuesday. Since you missed hearing him, I thought you might like to audit the class."

"I'd love to!" Melissa exclaimed. "What time shall I be there?"

"Class starts at eleven, but I'd get there earlier if I were you. A lot of people will be coming to hear him." Sean gave her the classroom number. "I'd save you a seat, but students get first crack at them, and our class is full."

"That's all right. I don't mind sitting in the back or even standing."

"You might have to," he warned. "If we miss each other in the crowd, we can have lunch afterward and discuss his lecture—if you have the time."

"I'm loaded with it at the moment."

"Good. Suppose we meet by the bench in the quad where we had coffee."

Melissa was revitalized by Sean's call. She hadn't realized how much she missed stimulating adult conversation. Even the prospect made her troubles seem less pressing.

She left the house early on Tuesday morning, but even so, the lecture hall was filled when she arrived. George Clement Williamson was world famous. Melissa gladly stood in the back of the hall throughout his lengthy lecture.

When she went to the quad afterward, Sean was already there. "It's a good thing we picked a meeting place," he remarked. "I looked around, but I didn't see you. What did you think of him?"

"I thought he was inspiring. I was especially impressed by his views on integrating nature with architecture whenever possible. Remember when builders used to simply bulldoze everything in their path?"

They sat on the bench discussing the lecture and exchanging views. Finally Sean glanced at his watch. "Shall we continue this over lunch? I have a class at two."

As they walked to the student union Melissa said, "I envy you. I wish I could have gotten into the summer session."

"That's funny, because I'd like to be in your shoes. I wouldn't mind being a beach bum for a couple of months, but I've wasted enough time already."

"I have, too," she answered soberly.

Sean turned his head to smile at her. "I have a few years on you."

"But you're in grad school." Melissa sighed. "It's so aggravating to have nothing to do all day when I could be working toward my degree."

He slanted a glance at her. "Taking care of the house and cooking for your husband must take up some of your time."

"Oh... well, yes, but Granger is out of town. On a business trip."

"Does he travel a lot?"

"This is the first long trip since we were married." Melissa was unaware of her woebegone expression.

"That's tough. Have you been married long?"

"Not very." She mustered a smile. "Well, everybody has problems." She changed the subject, not wanting to reveal too much about herself.

Sean didn't ask any more personal questions, but during lunch he made a suggestion. "If you have so much time on your hands, why don't you spend some of it here on campus?"

"Doing what?"

"You could drop in at the library, for one thing. I don't suppose you'd be allowed to check out books until you're an official student, but you could certainly use the reading room. Just browsing through the stacks is a revelation. The collection is tremendous."

"That *would* be interesting." Melissa's face lit up. "There are a lot of subjects I'd like to know more about. Like plant diseases and alternatives to pesticides."

"If you run across anything you want to study in depth, I could check it out for you on my card."

"That's awfully nice of you."

"Glad to do it. Two more places worth visiting are Melnitz Hall and the theater arts building. They both have theaters. One is for stage plays and the other shows films."

"I had no idea there was so much to do here besides attend classes," Melissa exclaimed.

"It's one alternative to boredom." Sean smiled.

"I'm going to follow all your suggestions," she declared. "You're a lifesaver. How can I ever thank you?"

"No thanks necessary. It will be nice to have someone to hang out with."

Melissa was afraid she'd given him the wrong impression. "This campus is so huge that our chances of running into each other are pretty slim," she said lightly.

"We can arrange to meet at our bench."

She certainly didn't want to hurt his feelings after he'd been so helpful, but a sticky situation could develop if she didn't set him straight. "I don't think that's a very good idea, Sean," she said carefully.

"It was a perfectly innocent suggestion," he said. "No ulterior motives. I enjoy your company and we have a lot in common. My classmates are all in their early or middle twenties. They speak a different language."

"I know. I expect to suffer culture shock." Melissa laughed.

"It's a lot easier if you have an ally to lapse into English with, but I didn't mean to make you uncomfortable. Forget I even mentioned it," he said pleasantly.

Melissa felt terrible at having misjudged him. The only remedy was to be completely honest. "I'm really sorry for thinking you were coming on to me, Sean. I should have known better."

His eyes twinkled. "Not necessarily. You're a very beautiful woman. Unfortunately for me, I draw the line at married women—especially when they have jealous husbands,'' he teased.

Melissa didn't want to think about Granger just then. ''Well, as long as we cleared that up, how about meeting for lunch tomorrow? Same time, same place.''

That day marked a turning point for Melissa. She stopped brooding about Granger and began enjoying life again, the way she used to. The days she spent on campus were absorbing, making the lonely nights a little easier to bear.

Granger noticed the improvement when he telephoned. ''What have you been doing with yourself? You sound different.''

''Probably because I stopped moping around and realized I had to develop some new interests,'' she answered.

''Like what?'' he asked suspiciously.

''I've been having the most fantastic time!''

She told him about the budding actors and actresses she'd watched perform, and the music students she was sure were destined for greatness. Melissa had spent hours exploring every facet of the sprawling university, and her excitement was evident in her voice.

Granger's voice was flat by comparison. ''It sounds as if you're living a full life without me.''

''Didn't you want me to?'' she asked coolly, reminded of her grievances.

''Why wouldn't I?'' he asked with equal reserve.

Melissa's happy mood dissolved. ''No reason. I'm sure it eases your conscience.''

''What do I have to feel guilty about? Have you been reading the tabloids again?'' he demanded. ''I was not

Crystal's date last weekend. We simply appeared together at a charity benefit for London orphans."

"I didn't happen to read about that, but it's nice to know you're bringing happiness to other people, too." Melissa was appalled at the acid in her voice, but she couldn't help herself. The pain of knowing Granger was slipping away from her was too devastating.

"What are you implying? That I'm have an affair with Crystal?"

"You said it, I didn't."

"You didn't have to. That's what you think."

"I'm not alone," Melissa answered bitterly. "Why else would those reporters cover you two like a blanket?"

"Because people like to read about us!" Granger shouted. He made an obvious effort to control himself. "The studio encourages publicity because it's good for the movie. They alert the press when we're going to appear somewhere."

"Even though you're a married man?"

"Responsible columnists don't suggest that Crystal and I are involved. They simply write about glamorous functions and who was there. That's what people are interested in—God knows why!"

"You're both very exciting," Melissa said in a small voice.

"I didn't think you shared that opinion," he answered. "What's happened to us, Melissa? How could you lose faith in me so easily?"

"You've been so detached lately," she said haltingly. "I get the feeling that you've gone back to your old world, and there's no place in it for me."

"You can't really believe that. Haven't I told you how much I miss you?"

"You don't say it with much conviction."

"Melissa, dear heart, what more can I do? I practically begged you to come with me."

"Not lately, though," she said forlornly. "You never mention it anymore."

"Because I know you aren't willing to leave Betsy, and I don't want to start an argument."

"I wasn't unwilling," Melissa protested. "I simply couldn't at the time. Even *you* understood that."

"But you were supposed to hire someone to replace Mrs. Flannery, and you haven't done it. What does that tell me?"

"You never asked whether I did or not," she exclaimed. "What message does that send *me?*"

"Are you saying you *have* found someone competent?" Excitement filled Granger's voice.

"I don't have to, that's the wonderful part." Melissa finally told him about the housekeeper's complete turnaround, and the reason for it.

When she'd finished he said, "That's really incredible. I'm sorry you all had such a traumatic experience, but this means you can join me."

"In a week or two. If you still want me," she added.

"How can you even ask such a question? If you only knew how much I miss you," he groaned. "I don't know how many more lonely nights I can take."

Melissa felt as if a great weight had been lifted from her heart. This was the old Granger, the man she loved.

"I keep remembering how you feel in my arms," he said huskily. "I dream that you're here with me, and when I wake up in an empty bed I want to get on a plane and come home."

"I wish you could," she whispered.

"I can't, but you can come to me. Ah, darling, I can hardly wait. I plan to take you to bed and keep you there for a week."

She laughed breathlessly. "I thought you were going to show me Europe."

"Eventually. First I'm going to make love to you for hours. I want to kiss you and hold you and touch you. I want to take off all your clothes and see you completely nude. Your body is so exquisite."

Melissa felt a spreading warmth in her midsection as she remembered *his* body. "Oh, Granger, it's been so long." She sighed.

"Too long," he answered forcefully. "Tell me what day you're coming and I'll make an airline reservation."

"I can't get away for at least a week. Mrs. Flannery has a doctor's appointment next Thursday. He's going to remove the bandage and see how the cut is healing."

"Surely you can plan to leave by then," Granger said impatiently.

"If all goes well. But there are a lot of things she can't do yet, like changing the beds and taking heavy pots off the stove. I help out, even though she doesn't like to have me lift a finger. Honestly, Granger, Mrs. Flannery is a different woman."

He was more interested in his wife than his housekeeper. "Why don't I make a reservation for you for Friday?"

Melissa chewed on her lower lip, torn between duty and desire. "Perhaps you'd better wait until after her appointment. I'll call you as soon as we get home."

"Damn it, Melissa, I'm as compassionate as the next guy, but I want you here with me!"

"Don't you think I want the same thing, darling?"

"Sometimes I wonder," he answered somberly.

"Please, Granger, we just got things straightened out. Let's don't argue again," she pleaded.

"You're right, angel," he said remorsefully. "It's just that I'm so frustrated by all the delays."

"It won't be much longer," she soothed.

"It better not be, or I don't know what I'll do."

"As long as you don't console yourself with Crystal." Melissa tried to keep her voice light.

"You have nothing to worry about there, I guarantee you. She's just a pal."

"I wish you didn't have such glamorous friends," Melissa remarked plaintively.

"None of them can compare to my gorgeous wife." His voice deepened. "I'll be counting the days until you get here."

Unfortunately Melissa wasn't able to leave for London in a week, as planned. Mrs. Flannery's hand wasn't healing as fast as the doctor had hoped. He did say she should be able to use it in another week, however.

Granger didn't take the news well. An argument was only narrowly averted. In the end, though, he was resigned to the delay.

Melissa wasn't any happier about it than Granger, but nothing could dampen her spirits. The prospect of seeing him again made the whole world rosy.

Sean commented on the change in her when they met for lunch one day. "What's happened to you lately? You act as if you won the lottery."

"Better than that." She smiled enchantingly. "I'm going to London soon to be with my husband."

Sean's eyebrow climbed. "When you said your husband was on a long trip, I didn't realize he was in Europe. What does he do?"

Melissa hesitated. "There are a couple of things I should tell you first. I haven't been completely honest about myself."

"Sounds ominous." He smiled. "What dark secret have you been hiding?"

"My name, for one thing. It isn't Melissa Fairfield, it's Melissa McMasters." When Sean stared at her blankly she said, "I'm married to Granger McMasters."

"The movie star?" Sean asked incredulously.

"Yes."

"Why the secrecy? Most women would shout it from the housetops."

"I didn't want my attendance here to become a media event. You have no idea how the press hounds Granger, and I'd be in for my share of it if the news got around."

"I guess I can understand that. But why are you telling me *me?*"

"I consider you a friend," she answered simply. "I know I can trust you."

"I'm honored. Overwhelmed, but honored." He laughed. "What other secrets have you been keeping?"

"Just that I was married before. Granger isn't the father of my child. Betsy is seven."

"I'll bet she's cute. I have nieces and nephews around her age."

"They do make life interesting."

"Unfortunately mine live back East. It's a lonely life without family, especially on the weekends."

Melissa couldn't quite swallow that. She'd noticed the admiring glances Sean had received from the coeds on campus. "I can't imagine a man like you sitting home alone on Saturday nights."

"You'd be surprised at how often," he replied wryly. "I know I should date more, but somehow the chemistry is never there."

"It will be when you meet the right girl," she said gently.

"I hope so." He smiled. "Everything on TV is a rerun."

"I have an idea. Tomorrow is Saturday. Why don't you come over in the afternoon for a swim, and then we'll barbecue."

Sean's face sobered. "That's very sweet of you, but I wasn't making a bid for sympathy."

"*I* am." Melissa grinned. "I'm tired of Saturday-night reruns, too, and Betsy loves company."

"Do you think your husband would mind?" he asked uncertainly.

"Of course not." Melissa's smile lit up her face. "We trust each other completely."

Sean and Betsy hit it off from the start. It was obvious that he liked children. After an initial evaluation period, Betsy followed him around like a puppy. Melissa's heart twisted as she realized how much her daughter missed Granger. He'd left a gap in both their lives.

Melissa and Betsy were already in the pool when Sean came out of the cabana in his bathing trunks. As he walked toward the diving board the telephone rang.

"Would you answer it?" Melissa called. "I told Mrs. Flannery to take a rest."

"Sure." He made a detour and picked up the phone.

"Who is this?" Granger asked sharply when he heard a male voice.

"Sean Crosley. Is this Mr. McMasters?" Sean recognized his voice.

"Yes. May I speak to my wife?" Granger asked grimly.

"Just a moment. It's your husband," Sean called to Melissa.

"It's Mac!" Betsy shouted. "I want to talk to him first." She scrambled out of the pool and grabbed the receiver. "Hi, Mac, when are you coming home?"

"Not for a few weeks, I'm afraid." Granger managed to mask his tension. "I miss you, honey. What have you been up to? Are you practicing your diving like I showed you?"

"Yes, but I still get water up my nose. Sean says he can teach me how to breathe. He's Mom's friend from school."

"I know who he is," Granger muttered. "Let me talk to your mother."

"But I haven't told you about Clancy yet. Sean says he could be a show dog if we started training him. Wouldn't that be neat? Sean knows about a whole bunch of things. He's been all over the world."

Melissa had gotten out of the pool and paused to dry her hands and face, giving Betsy a chance to talk to her beloved Mac. Finally she couldn't wait any longer.

Taking the receiver from Betsy, she said breathlessly, "Hi, darling. I didn't expect to hear from you this early."

"Obviously, or you wouldn't have let your boyfriend answer the phone," Granger said tautly.

Her smile faded. "How can you say things like that when you know they aren't true?"

"You *are* entertaining a man, aren't you?"

"That sounds so ugly," she protested. "Sean is a guest. I invited him over for a swim. What's so terrible about that? Betsy and Mrs. Flannery are here, too."

"He seems to be a big hit with the whole family. Betsy is very impressed with him."

"She misses you, Granger. Betsy is just hungry for male companionship."

"The same holds true for you, I suppose," he answered icily.

"Nobody could ever take your place," she said quietly.

Granger's voice softened. "I'm sorry I blew my stack, angel, but I'm really not happy about having you invite this guy over. You don't know anything about him. He's just someone who picked you up."

"It wasn't like that at all. Actually I guess you could say I picked *him* up." She laughed. "Anyway, we've gotten to know each other since then."

"Where?"

"Sean was the one who told me about all the fascinating things to do at U.C.L.A. I meet him there for lunch or coffee very often. We've become good friends."

"That explains a lot of things. Like the reason you're so reluctant to leave Los Angeles."

"That's not true! There's nothing I'd like more."

"You could have fooled me. Every time I try to pin you down, you have another excuse."

"You're not being fair. You know perfectly well why I can't leave."

"I'm beginning to have an inkling."

"You're acting like a spoiled child." Melissa was starting to lose patience. "I can't simply walk out on my obligations."

"Too bad I'm not one of them," Granger remarked sarcastically.

"What do you want from me?" she asked in frustration. "You know I had a child to consider. Betsy was the reason you married me."

"No, she was the reason *you* married *me.* I lost sight of that fact."

"I'm sorry if you feel I'm not fulfilling my part of the bargain," she said stiffly. Melissa always felt pain when she was reminded of why Granger had married her.

"I wouldn't say that," he drawled. "I think we both got what we were looking for."

"Evidently not, or you wouldn't be throwing such a tantrum," she said bitterly.

"I'm a territorial sort of guy. I get annoyed when someone encroaches on my property."

"That's a chauvinist thing to say!" she flared.

"You're correct. I don't own you. We have a mutually convenient arrangement with no strings attached. You were right to remind me."

"That's not what I meant," she said in a small voice.

"Why not tell it like it is? We've never pretended ours was a great love affair."

Tears clogged Melissa's throat, but she fought them back. "I still wouldn't want you to get the wrong idea about why I invited Sean here today."

"I'm sure you wouldn't carry on in front of Betsy." Granger's anger had dissipated and he sounded as if he'd lost interest in the entire subject. "Well, I'll let you get back to them."

"Wait, Granger! Do you still want me to come to London next week?"

"That's entirely up to you. I know it's difficult for you, so don't feel you have to come. I'll be back in a few weeks, anyway."

Melissa hung up, feeling as though the bottom had dropped out of her world. She could understand and deal with Granger's anger, but not his indifference. How had things gone so wrong, so suddenly? Was Sean really the cause of this quarrel, or was he just a convenient smoke screen?

"Mom, aren't you coming in the pool?" Betsy called.

Melissa wanted to go somewhere and hide, like a small, wounded animal. But she couldn't. Forcing her taut body to relax, she pinned a smile on her face and walked over to the pool.

Sean swept the wet hair out of his eyes and looked up at her. "Is everything okay?"

"Couldn't be better." Her facial muscles felt tight from the determined effort.

The following week was the worst one of Melissa's life. Granger didn't phone for three days, and when he finally did call, it was like talking to a casual friend. He was pleasant, but impersonal. He asked about Betsy and Mrs. Flannery, and Melissa asked how the movie was progressing. As usual, Granger concluded the call by saying he missed her, but it was clearly a ritual remark. He didn't ask about her plans for London. Under the circumstances, Melissa didn't bring up the subject, either.

After what had happened, U.C.L.A. no longer held any charm. Nothing did. She spent hours wandering around the garden, wondering how to break through the wall Granger had erected between them.

Mrs. Flannery watched in concern as Melissa skipped lunch day after day and only picked at her dinner. "Mr. McMasters will be home soon," she said gently, misunderstanding the reason for her desolation.

"I know." Melissa forced a smile.

"You really should get out more," the older woman urged. "It would make the time pass faster."

"You're probably right," Melissa agreed.

When she didn't act on the suggestion, Mrs. Flannery invented little errands to get her out of the house. One day she sent her to the grocery store.

"I intend to give that manager a piece of my mind," the housekeeper said. "They forgot to send the buns I ordered, and I promised Betsy hamburgers for dinner. Will you go to the store for me?"

Melissa agreed listlessly. She drove to the supermarket instead of the specialty market they usually patronized, because the chain store was closer.

While she was waiting in line at the checkout stand, Melissa glanced at the magazine rack. Granger's name leapt out at her from the front page of a tabloid newspaper. Underneath the bold headline was a picture of him holding a woman in his arms.

Melissa reached for the paper with a feeling of doom. The headline read: "Is the marriage over? Superstar caught romancing another woman."

She paid for her groceries in a numbed state. Her fears had been justified. But how ironic that Crystal wasn't the one she needed to worry about.

In the privacy of her car, Melissa read about her husband and an actress named Shelley Blair. A reporter had trailed them to a little out-of-the-way restaurant where they'd obviously hoped nobody would see them. There weren't many details, but Melissa didn't need any. She'd seen that tender look on Granger's face directed at her when she was the one in favor.

How could he explain away this direct evidence? Not that she intended to ask him about it. Their marriage was clearly over. The reason for all the arguments and tension between them lately was now clear. Granger wanted out of their marriage, but he didn't know how to tell her.

His fit of temper that Saturday wasn't over Sean. Granger was merely rebelling at an intolerable situation.

Melissa drove home slowly, trying to deal with all the problems ahead. She would have to find an apartment and see if she could get her old customers back. Although, the three days a week at Granger's had provided most of her income. He would undoubtedly offer to pay alimony, but she had no intention of accepting any. Without Granger's help she might have lost Betsy. That was payment enough.

Melissa knew that Betsy would be terribly upset over the divorce, so she postponed telling her until it became necessary. She wouldn't have shared her plans with Mrs. Flannery, either, but the older woman kept urging her to go to London. Finally in desperation, Melissa told her the marriage was over.

Mrs. Flannery was appalled. "You can't leave because of a picture in one of those dreadful papers! I'm sure there's some explanation."

"It isn't only that." Melissa didn't care to divulge the reason Granger had married her. "He wants his freedom, and I'm giving it to him."

"That's stuff and nonsense! Mr. Mac adores you. I always knew it, even when I wouldn't admit it to myself."

"Maybe he did in the beginning, but you told me yourself that he was always that way with somebody new."

"I was a mean-spirited old woman. You know how wrong I was about everything."

Mrs. Flannery cited instances of Granger's thoughtfulness and generosity, rubbing salt into Melissa's already-raw wounds. She didn't have to be told how wonderful he was. But he didn't want her anymore. Melissa was emotionally drained when she finally ended the conversation.

To escape from the woman's determined efforts to change her mind, Melissa left the house early the next morning with the classified section of the newspaper. She'd put off looking for an apartment, reluctant to finalize her decision. But Mrs. Flannery had provided the impetus.

It proved to be a long, miserable day. All of the apartments in Melissa's price range were small and dreary. The neighborhoods were often run-down as well. Nothing she saw was even remotely acceptable.

Melissa was scraping bottom when she returned home, and she still had to face Mrs. Flannery's newest barrage of arguments. The housekeeper surprised her, however. She didn't mention Granger, either directly or indirectly. Maybe she'd finally resigned herself, Melissa hoped wearily.

Betsy made up for Mrs. Flannery that night. She never stopped talking about Granger. Every other sentence was about something they'd done together in the past, or somewhere she wanted him to take her as soon as he came home.

Melissa was exhausted when she went to her own room after Betsy was finally tucked into bed. All she wanted to do was take a bath and go to bed.

The warm bath was relaxing. When her eyelids started to droop she got out of the tub, wrapped herself in a towel and went into the bedroom barefoot. Her drowsiness was replaced by shock as she stared at the man standing in the middle of the room. It was Granger!

"How did you get here?" she whispered, unsure if she was hallucinating.

"I phoned this morning while you were out. After Mrs. Flannery told me you were leaving me, I caught the first plane home." His expression was unreadable. "Didn't you think I deserved a chance to defend myself?"

"It isn't necessary." Melissa glanced away quickly as a wave of longing swept over her. Granger was even more breathtakingly handsome than she remembered.

"It obviously *is* necessary if you feel you have grounds for divorce."

"We had an agreement," she murmured. "Before we got married I told you I'd give you your freedom if you ever wanted it."

"Why didn't you wait until I asked?"

"I wanted to make it easier for you."

"How very generous! It couldn't be that *you* wanted a divorce?"

"You don't have to spare my feelings," Melissa said in a low voice. "I don't want you to feel guilty that our marriage didn't work out."

"You're the one who decided that."

"No, I'm the one who's honest enough to admit it. All we do lately is argue," she said hopelessly. "I finally realized it's because you feel trapped."

"You've never known how I feel," he said quietly.

"Not recently, that's obvious." She sighed.

"We have to talk, Melissa."

"I'd rather not." She couldn't bear to listen to Granger apologize for not loving her. "You've been very good to Betsy and me. I'll always be grateful to you."

"I never wanted gratitude," he answered forcefully.

"I know that. You're a very giving person. I hope we can continued to be friends after..." She swallowed hard, unable to go on.

"How can I settle for that?" He grasped her shoulders and jerked her toward him. "I love you, Melissa. I can't let you go."

She stared up at him in a daze. "You never said you loved me."

"I was afraid I'd scare you away. You were so adamant about not getting emotionally involved. I knew you only married me for Betsy's sake, but we were happy together." His voice held a pleading note. "Don't leave me, sweetheart."

"I thought you'd be relieved." Melissa couldn't believe she'd heard him correctly. "You've been so indifferent toward me lately. You practically told me not to come to London."

"I was so jealous of your friend, Sean, that I acted like a class-A jerk," he said disgustedly.

"Was that why you started seeing Shelley Blair?" Melissa asked soberly.

"I only saw her that one night, and it isn't the way it looks. Shelley is just an old friend. We made a couple of movies together years ago, but her career is on the skids. She's had trouble getting parts lately."

"I'd prefer not to hear about her."

"You have to listen to me," he said urgently. "Shelley had been promised a part in a London play, but when she got there, they'd cast someone else. She'd read that I was in London, so she called me, badly in need of consolation. I knew what the tabloids would make of it, so I took her to a little restaurant off the beaten track. Unfortunately we were followed. Those vultures never let up," Granger said with distaste. "I'm only sorry that you were dragged into their sordid story."

"It doesn't matter." The true story was so simple that Melissa was almost giddy with relief.

"You were going to leave me, anyway?" His face was drawn.

"Not by choice. I was crushed when I thought you were tired of me."

He gazed at her with dawning excitement. "You really cared? It wasn't just your pride that was hurt?"

Full realization had finally taken hold. Granger loved her! She reached up to clasp her arms around his neck. "We've done a rotten job of communicating. I think I fell in love with you that first day, when you pulled me out of your pool."

A brilliant smile chased the strain from Granger's face. "You certainly managed to keep it a secret."

"No more than you did. I suffered every time I saw a picture of you and Crystal together."

"No other woman has meant anything to me since the first day you came into my life." He folded her into a convulsive embrace. "My dearest love, you don't know what I went through when I thought I lost you."

She smoothed his hair tenderly. "I do know, believe me."

"I was so afraid you wouldn't be here when I got home. The flight was agony."

"How were you able to get away in the middle of the picture?" she asked.

"Nothing could have kept me there. You're more important than a hundred movies," he said in a throbbing voice.

"You have to go back, though, don't you?"

"Unfortunately." He sighed. "A lot of people's jobs depend on me or I'd never consider it. Will you wait for me just a little longer, darling?"

"I'll do better than that," she said softly. "I'll go back with you."

"That's what I was hoping you'd say." Granger's kiss expressed all the pent-up yearning of the past weeks.

While his mouth possessed hers fiercely, his hands roamed restlessly over her body. Gradually he became aware of the fact that Melissa was only wrapped in a towel. He found the corner that was tucked in and tugged it free. When he loosened his embrace slightly, the towel dropped to the floor. She was gloriously nude in his arms.

Granger's caresses over the length of her body made Melissa purr with delight. She unbuttoned his shirt and moved sensuously against him, accentuating the pleasure. His expression was molten as he swung her into his arms and started toward the bed, gazing deeply into her eyes.

"I've been sleeping alone too long," he said in a throaty voice. "Tonight will be a dream come true."

Melissa smiled enchantingly. "You might not get much sleep."

"I'm counting on just the opposite," he murmured.

*   *   *   *   *

Silhouette Special Edition

COMING NEXT MONTH

#751 HEARTBREAK HANK—Myrna Temte *Cowboy Country*
Principal Emily Franklin was meeting with local bad boy Hank Dawson to
discuss his daughter's schoolwork. But when the meetings continued,
rumors raged—had the rodeo star lassoed the learned lady?

#752 AMAZING GRACIE—Victoria Pade
Gabe Duran collected antiques; his new neighbor Gracie Canon restored
them. Desire for the same collection had them fighting over something
old; desire of another kind had them trying something new....

#753 SWISS BLISS—Bevlyn Marshall
Consultant Susan Barnes had jetted to the Alps on business. Brusque
Swiss hotel owner Maximillian Kaiser was as corporate as they
came...until passion burst in—without an appointment!

#754 THERE AND NOW—Linda Lael Miller *Beyond the Threshold*
When Elisabeth McCartney appeared in 1892, the townspeople called her
a witch. Jonathan Fortner called her the love of his life. How could she
tell him a lifetime lay between them?

#755 MAN WITHOUT A PAST—Laurie Paige
Sutter Kinnard was determined not to disappoint the woman he'd
protected like a sister. But Meredith Lawton's dream of a perfect marriage
was a terrifying challenge to a man without a past....

#756 BRIDE ON THE LOOSE—Debbie Macomber
Those Manning Men
Straitlaced secretary Charlotte Weston was mortified! Her teenage
daughter had tried to bribe Jason Manning, their laid-back landlord, into
asking Charlotte out. He'd honorably refused...and made the dinner
date for free...!

AVAILABLE THIS MONTH:

#745 SILENT SAM'S SALVATION
Myrna Temte

**#746 DREAMBOAT OF THE
WESTERN WORLD**
Tracy Sinclair

#747 BEYOND THE NIGHT
Christine Flynn

**#748 WHEN SOMEBODY
LOVES YOU**
Trisha Alexander

#749 OUTCAST WOMAN
Lucy Gordon

#750 ONE PERFECT ROSE
Emilie Richards

Take 4 bestselling love stories FREE

Plus get a FREE surprise gift!

Summer romance has never been so hot!

SILHOUETTE

SUMMER Sizzlers™

A collection of hot summer reading by three of
Silhouette's hottest authors:

**Ann Major
Paula Detmer Riggs
Linda Lael Miller**

Put some sizzle into your summer reading. You
won't want to miss your ticket to summer fun—with
the best summer reading under the sun!

FREE GIFT OFFER

To receive your free gift, send us the specified number of proofs-of-purchase from any specially marked Free Gift Offer Harlequin or Silhouette book with the Free Gift Certificate properly completed, plus a check or money order (do not send cash) to cover postage and handling payable to Harlequin/Silhouette Free Gift Promotion Offer. We will send you the specified gift.

FREE GIFT CERTIFICATE

ITEM	A. GOLD TONE EARRINGS	B. GOLD TONE BRACELET	C. GOLD TONE NECKLACE
# of proofs-of-purchase required	3	6	9
Postage and Handling	$1.75	$2.25	$2.75
Check one	☐	☐	☐

Name: _____

Address: _____

City: _____ State: _____ Zip Code: _____

Mail this certificate, specified number of proofs-of-purchase and a check or money order for postage and handling to: HARLEQUIN/SILHOUETTE FREE GIFT OFFER 1992, P.O. Box 9057, Buffalo, NY 14269-9057. Requests must be received by July 31, 1992.

PLUS—Every time you submit a completed certificate with the correct number of proofs-of-purchase, you are automatically entered in our MILLION DOLLAR SWEEPSTAKES! No purchase or obligation necessary to enter. See below for alternate means of entry and how to obtain complete sweepstakes rules.

MILLION DOLLAR SWEEPSTAKES
NO PURCHASE OR OBLIGATION NECESSARY TO ENTER

To enter, hand-print (mechanical reproductions are not acceptable) your name and address on a 3″×5″ card and mail to Million Dollar Sweepstakes 6097, c/o either P.O. Box 9056, Buffalo, NY 14269-9056 or P.O. Box 621, Fort Erie, Ontario L2A 5X3. Limit: one entry per envelope. Entries must be sent via 1st-class mail. For eligibility, entries must be received no later than March 31, 1994. No liability is assumed for printing errors, lost, late or misdirected entries.

Sweepstakes is open to persons 18 years of age or older. All applicable laws and regulations apply. Sweepstakes offer void wherever prohibited by law. Prizewinners will be determined no later than May 1994. Chances of winning are determined by the number of entries distributed and received. For a copy of the Official Rules governing this sweepstakes offer, send a self-addressed, stamped envelope (WA residents need not affix return postage) to: Million Dollar Sweepstakes Rules, P.O. Box 4733, Blair, NE 68009.

✂ **SS3U**

ONE PROOF-OF-PURCHASE

To collect your fabulous FREE GIFT you must include the necessary FREE GIFT proofs-of-purchase with a properly completed offer certificate.

(See inside back cover for offer details)